BEN BRAVER AND THE INCREDIBLE EXPLODING KID

Don't miss
The Super Life of Ben Braver!

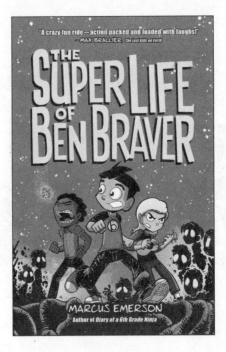

"Fans of superhero fiction will laugh out loud and identify with aggressively regular Ben. Just the right mix of mystery and kooky fun."

— *Kirkus Reviews*

"A clever hybrid novel that's sure to be a hit with the comic-cartoon crowd and fans of superhero tales."

— *School Library Journal*

BEN BRAVER AND THE INCREDIBLE EXPLODING KID

By

Marcus Emerson

SQUARE FISH

ROARING BROOK PRESS

New York

SQUARE
FISH

An imprint of Macmillan Publishing Group, LLC
120 Broadway, New York, NY 10271
mackids.com

Our books may be purchased in bulk for promotional, educational, or business use.
Please contact your local bookseller or the Macmillan Corporate and Premium
Sales Department at (800) 221-7945 ext. 5442 or by email at
MacmillanSpecialMarkets@macmillan.com.

Library of Congress Control Number: 2018944887

ISBN 978-1-250-23341-7 (paperback)   ISBN 978-1-250-14327-3 (ebook)

Originally published in the United States by Roaring Brook Press
First Square Fish edition, 2020
Square Fish logo designed by Filomena Tuosto

1   3   5   7   9   10   8   6   4   2

AR: 4.1 / LEXILE: 590L

. . . FOR MY SISTER, KRISSY

PROLOGUE

Sixty miles per hour.

The top speed of a Vespa scooter.

I'm not a doctor, but I don't think sixty miles an hour is fast enough to outrun an exploding atom bomb.

Headmaster Kepler was riding passenger, shouting instructions on how to "operate a vehicle," his words.

"I know how to drive a scooter!" I shouted, cranking the Vespa's handle so hard that it snapped. "Oh, farts . . ."

So there we were, coasting on a dying scooter, seconds away from an atomic explosion that would take out Kepler Academy and the city of Lost Nation.

I can confidently say that was the worst day of my short, little life.

Thousands were about to die.

All my friends were about to die.

I was about to die.

And it was 100 percent my fault. . . .

CHAPTER ONE

Sunday.

Six months earlier.

I sat alone in the passenger seat of a self-driving Volkswagen Beetle.

Summer was over, and I was headed back to Kepler Academy—a super secret school for kids with superpowers.

It was like the X-Mansion, but without all the spandex.

A whole summer had passed since I saved the academy from an army of plant people created by a woman named Abigail Cutter.

She was all kinds of crazy.

With a loogie, some dirt, and a strand of your hair, Abigail could grow your evil twin, which she controlled with her mind.

They were horrifying plant zombies who ate earthworms by the handful, or as the greatest scientific minds called them, worm-eaters.

Premium-grade nightmare fuel.

My car had been driving all day, so the school had to be close. It should've been all Colorado mountains and trees outside my window.

But it wasn't.

An empty desert wasteland stretched out for miles on all sides of me.

"Computer, where am I?" I asked.

The GPS didn't answer because I don't live in a *Star Trek* movie.

The clock showed 1 a.m.

"Flippin' eggs, are you serious?" I muttered.

I should've been at Kepler Academy hours ago! What was my car thinking driving through the desert at *one in the stupid idiot morning*?

The VW sputtered to a stop. The headlights died slowly, leaving me alone in the dark. My door unlocked and popped open by itself.

I looked for the North Star, but it was cloudy. My dad and I have this thing—whenever I'm scared, all I have to do is find that star. We both look at it every night; it's like our way of saying "I miss you" to each other even if we're in different places.

Doesn't work when it's cloudy, though.

I stared at the empty desert outside my car.

And that's when I heard it—the sloppy, chomping sounds of worm-eaters.

I grabbed the edge of the car door to shut it, but instead of metal . . . I felt somebody's fingers.

Worm-eaters burst from the darkness, sprinting toward me. No screams. No grunts. Just moist feet slapping the dry desert crust.

The hand at my door grabbed my wrist and yanked me into the air until I was face-to-face with her.

It was Abigail Cutter.

Mangled worms fell from her nasty, chapped lips as her fingers morphed into thick vines that slithered around my neck, suffocating me.

I shot forward, eyes shut, drenched in cold sweat, screaming at the top of my lungs. I tried to push Abigail away, but when I opened my eyes . . .

She was gone.

I was still in my bed at home.

I'll say it again: nightmare fuel.

. . . What the jibs was wrong with me?

I pushed the blankets aside and looked out my window. Still black, but that's how it is when you need to get on the road by 4 a.m.

Mom flipped on the light. "Oh, good, you're up! Your car's outside!" she said, excited for my second year at Kepler Academy. Way more excited than I was.

When I left the academy last year, I was the baddest hero ever, but all that disappeared once I got home.

Every time I closed my eyes at night, I saw worm-eaters. I spent most nights wide awake, staring at my door until the sun came up.

My parents didn't know about the nightmares.

Or much of anything that happened last year.

Including the fact that I was powerless—the *only* powerless kid at Kepler Academy.

They asked me all summer to spill the beans, but all I ever said was, *"It was fun,"* because saying, *"I jumped off a ten-story building to save the school from a Godzilla-size plant zombie,"* would've given them a panic attack.

Or maybe it would've given *me* one.

I had spent the last three months dodging their questions by mowing lawns morning till night, every single day.

The work helped keep my mind off worm-eaters, and I liked the extra cash, too. I thought about blowing it all on a mountain of peanut butter cups, but instead I saved up and bought myself something nice.

After getting dressed and scraping a toothbrush across my teeth, I went outside.

Mom stood by the Kepler car as Dad tossed my bags into the trunk.

"That'll do it," Dad said, messing my hair up. "Don't come home this time without a power!"

I knew he was joking—that he only said it because he believed I already had come back with a power.

. . . joke's on him though, right?

Ugh.

Mom knelt and gave me a hug, but I just stood there like a stiff doll.

She pulled back. "Are you all right?"

"I guess," I said, but she saw through me.

"Hey, it'll be okay. You've already done this once. Going back will be like riding a bike. Once you're there, you'll hardly miss home at all."

"Even though we'll be missing *you* like crazy," Dad added.

I didn't want them to know I was scared, but I wasn't good at hiding it.

Mom hugged me tighter. "I know this is hard for you, but you need to know that it's harder for me. I don't want you to go, Ben. I want you to stay here and go to a boring school and sit around our boring house at night, but we both know you can't."

Dad put his hand on my head while I squeezed my mom.

"But . . . I'm scared," I said honestly.

Mom smiled. "Nothing wrong with that. I'm scared, too. Scared that something terrible will happen to you while you're gone."

Like jumping off a ten-story building.

"Being scared just means you get to be brave," Mom said. "Because we both know you have to go back. You belong there. People spend their entire lives looking for a greater destiny, but yours knocked at our door and invited you to come out to play. We might not know exactly why yet, but you *belong* at *that* school."

She was right.

I had to go back.

For her.

For my dad.

For all the students at the academy.

I was the hero who saved the school last year.

And what kind of hero goes into hiding after something like that?

CHAPTER TWO

Fourteen hours later, my car was driving through downtown Lost Nation, the city in the valley below Kepler Academy. Or, at least, below where the academy *used* to be.

A woman's voice with a British accent said I was five minutes away from my sequel—the *new* Kepler Academy.

Over the summer, I got a letter stating that the school had burned down. The building was a giant log cabin ski lodge, so it was basically made out of firewood. Nobody was hurt, but the building was beyond repair.

And after all I did to save it from destruction last year.

Go figure.

The letter also said that ninety-five-year-old Headmaster Donald Kepler had stepped down because of health reasons and that Vice Principal Raymond Archer would replace him.

I mean, those aren't tiny changes, like a new paint job or something. Those were *King Kong*–size changes.

It almost felt like starting over *again*.

So that's where I was headed—to the *new* Kepler Academy, which was apparently somewhere in the butt of Lost Nation.

My car turned corner after corner, each street darker than the last, until I was finally on a brick road with flickering streetlamps and some shady-looking people.

An old hag was pushing a grocery cart full of live chickens, a small group of punk rockers was break-dancing on cardboard, and a short dude wearing an Elvis Presley mask while taking a Polaroid selfie was on a staircase outside a dive called "Campion's Diner."

The GPS said I still had about four miles until my destination. Each mile that passed grew bleaker and bleaker.

Finally, my car pulled up to a metal garage door on a warehouse that looked abandoned. Actually, all the buildings on the street looked abandoned.

The garage door opened automatically, and my car drove forward, passing a long line of other parked Beetles, until coming to a full stop in front of a goat that stared at me with creepy, horizontal eyes.

There are so many *"what the heck?"* moments in my life—surprisingly, this wasn't one of them.

My car door unlocked, and I stepped out with my backpack. "S'up, man?"

The goat bobbed his head. "S'up."

He was a friend from last year. His name was Totes, and he was a graduate of Kepler Academy. His superpower was that he transformed into a goat, full time–style.

Not everyone develops *useful* powers.

Totes went to the trunk and swung my bags onto his back, then he took the lead. "Follow me."

We went to an elevator in a dark corner of the warehouse.

"Is the school on the second floor?" I asked.

"Nope. We're not goin' up," Totes said. "We're goin' *down*."

"*Underground?*" I sighed.

The goat pushed the basement button with his snout. The doors closed, and the elevator dropped.

A life without windows.

A life of canned food.

A life of concrete walls.

At the end of the year, I'll climb out of a hole squinting because I forgot what the sun looks like.

The elevator jerked to a stop. The doors opened half an inch and got stuck, but it was enough to let the sound of screaming kids seep in.

The horror!

Students were in agony!

Pain and suffering!

I tried to peek through the slit, but Totes got in the way.

"Dumb doors," he said, pushing his head against them. *"Every! Single! Time! Today!"*

The goat leaped forward, ramming his horns against the metal.

The doors clunked and then slid wide open.

A blast of cold air pushed into the elevator. My jaw dropped, and I couldn't believe my eyes.

". . . What the junk?" I whispered.

CHAPTER THREE

All I could do was stare.

On the other side of the elevator doors was the old Kepler Academy, still standing, and still outside.

The school had never burned down.

The story was a lie!

Totes dumped my bags onto the grass. "Ben Braver," he said.

"Ben Braver," a familiar voice repeated. "Check him off."

I stepped out of the elevator and felt the soft earth under my sneakers.

Raymond Archer, the new headmaster, was off to my side, wearing a wrinkle-free Hawaiian shirt.

Joel, the kid who could open portals the size of a quarter, stood next to him, checking off names on a clipboard.

"That's the last of them," Headmaster Archer said. "You can close your portal now, Joel."

Joel went to the elevator doors behind me. His glowing portal was propped open using long plastic tent poles, the ones that folded up when you wanted to put them away.

He yanked on one of the poles, popping it out of place.

The rest fell to the ground, and the portal instantly closed.

"I get extra cred for this, right?" Joel asked.

"A job well done is its own reward, and you've done your job well. Just remember, no *unauthorized* portals," Headmaster Archer said as he took Joel's clipboard. "And welcome back, Mr. Braver! Good to see you!" he shouted over his shoulder as he walked off.

"Cool trick," I said.

Joel shrugged. "I learned to stretch open my portals over the summer. Did you learn anything new with your power?"

"Nope," I quickly answered. "I'm still at the exact same level as I was last year."

Technically, that wasn't a lie.

I scanned for my friends but didn't see them.

Instead, I saw students using their powers right out in the open—a *gigantic* no-no at the academy.

Teachers ordered them to stop, but nobody listened. And there was no sign of Headmaster Kepler—I mean, *former* headmaster—anywhere. I wondered if he'd even be at the school this year.

Coach Lindsay Andrews was outside, too, defeated and sitting with the statue of Brock.

Man, school hadn't even started yet and the new head of security's spirits were crushed.

Everyone squealed as rain started pouring from gray clouds that someone had conjured up. A lightning bolt flashed along with the loudest crack of thunder I'd ever heard.

I stumbled back. My foot slipped in the wet grass, and I went down a short slope like it was a Slip 'N Slide.

When I stopped, everything vanished.

Like, *literally* everything.

The school. The students. All of it was gone.

The only thing left was a pile of ash where the Lodge used to be.

This was one of those *"what the heck?"* moments.

One second I was at school—the next second I was all alone in the mountains. Did I accidentally slip into another dimension or something?

I saw shapes in the forest moving like worm-eaters coming to life.

I started freaking out.

Like, blurry vision, woozy head freaking out.

That's when my best friend's head appeared.

It was Noah Nichols.

But it was *just* his head, floating four and a half feet off the ground.

I lost it.

I pulled my hair and screamed.

The rest of Noah's body suddenly appeared like he walked through an invisible wall. "Dude, chill! It's just me!" he said, grabbing my shoulders.

"Where'd everything go?"

"Everything's still here! You're just outside the holographic barrier!"

"The what?"

Noah pushed me back up the slope. The school, the stormy clouds, and the rowdy students magically reappeared.

Penny and Jordan were there, too.

PENNY PLUM
WITH THE POWER OF CONTROLLING MICE BY USING HER TRUSTY UKULELE!

NOAH NICHOLS
WITH THE POWER OF CREATING FIRE, BUT ONLY AFTER HE EATS BEEF JERKY!

AND **JORDAN...**
UM, I ACTUALLY DON'T KNOW JORDAN'S LAST NAME. I'M GONNA GO WITH JORDAN JACOB JINGLEHEIMER SCHMIDT UNTIL SOMEONE TELLS ME IT'S NOT THAT.

"Dude, compose," Penny said. "Everybody's looking!"

I clenched my teeth and sucked air through my nose until my hands stopped trembling.

"Check it out," Noah said, pointing at a line of tripods behind us. "They're holopods. They cover the school with a giant hologram of a burned-down building. It's camouflage. *Super* rad."

"Are you all right?" Penny asked. "You look a little . . . sick. You're not gonna chuck, are you?"

"No, I just . . ." I said. "I'm fine."

But I wasn't fine.

I knew I was scared, but I didn't know I was *that* scared.

That didn't bode well for the rest of my year.

CHAPTER FOUR

10 p.m.

Later that night.

After a lame *"Welcome Back!"* reception with a dinner fit for a funeral, kids spent the rest of the night unpacking in their rooms.

Students keep the same dorm until they graduate, so Noah and I were roomies for life, and Penny was still right upstairs again.

Jordan bunked with us, too, because his alternative would've been rooming with Dexter Dunn, my very own personal bully.

Even though I hated him, Dexter's kind of the reason I was at the school to begin with. He was my neighbor back at home and almost killed me once, which is actually what brought Headmaster Kepler to my house to invite me to the academy.

So I guess Dexter's not *all* bad?

Penny hacked away at the small hole in our ceiling that Noah had made last year with a fireball burp. It was almost big enough for her to climb through now.

"You sure you know what you're doing?" Noah asked.

Penny hung upside down through the hole. "Not even a little bit."

"Did any of you see Headmaster Kepler outside?" I asked.

"No," Jordan said. "He's probably livin' it up in Cancún right about now."

"Doubt it," Penny said. "He stepped down *'due to health reasons.'*"

"Maybe that's a good thing then," I said. "It means we can investigate the mystery of Fifteen without worrying about him catching us."

The first class at Kepler Academy had only fourteen superpowered students. Everyone knew that. It was taught in history class.

Except it wasn't true.

At the end of last year, we found a photo that showed *fifteen* students instead. The headmaster had it hidden away in his creepy cave of secrets in the forest.

WHICH ONE IS FIFTEEN?

A cave *overflowing* with fake articles about full-blown superheroes, some villain named the Reaper, and the end of the world.

There was even a weird police mug shot of the headmaster, like he was some kind of villain.

But he isn't—at least, I don't think he is.

Penny had taken pics of everything with her phone for evidence, but we still didn't have any leads.

"Did you ask your parents about Fifteen?" I asked her.

"Yeah, but they didn't know anything," Penny said. "Which doesn't surprise me."

"Unless their memories were wiped," Jordan said. "Kepler has people for that."

"That's just something he says," Penny said. "I think we'd know if any of us had our brains wiped."

"But we *wouldn't* know because our brains were scrubbed," Noah said.

"Fine, then *I'd* know," Penny insisted.

They agreed to disagree, mostly because nobody wanted to argue all night since school started the next morning.

Everyone said good night and fell asleep pretty much right away.

Everyone except me.

I stared at shadows, afraid that plant zombies would steal my body in the middle of the night.

Some hero I was.

Time crawled as the moon inched across my window.

Five hours I stared into the dark, until I heard a sputtering outside.

I froze.

It couldn't have been a worm-eater, right?

They don't sputter. Go-carts sputter. Garbage disposals sputter. Butts sputter.

I slipped out of bed and army-crawled to the window. Slowly, I slid it open.

In the street was an old Vespa scooter, engine sputtering, with the rider standing in front of it.

Was I dreaming?

Was there really a Vespa ninja outside?

The biker's helmet turned toward the forest.

I looked, too, but the trees were too dark to see anything.

Please don't be worm-eaters.

She hopped onto her scooter and zipped off in a hurry.

She saw something in the trees.

She must have.

And then I saw Dexter and Vic stumble out, drag-
ging their feet like zombies.

This couldn't be happening!

They stopped next to the statue of Brock. Vic put his
hand to his mouth and loudly slurped something out
of it.

Worms!

It was dark out, but I could see worms falling out of the goth-wannabe's mouth!

Dexter was eating them, too!

Suddenly Vic's head snapped in my direction.

I ducked.

They're not really worm-eaters. My eyes are lying to me because they hate me! This is all just a really bad dream!

The wet sound of chewing worms grew louder in my ears as I crawled back into bed and pulled the covers over my face.

C'mon, brain! Wake up already!

Penny's chainsaw snore ripped through the hole in the ceiling, and I remembered the look on her face when she was taken by Abigail last year.

It wasn't just me who was in danger. It was Penny. It was Noah and Jordan. It was the whole school.

Dexter and Vic slurped again.

That was it.

Operation Save the Day was in full swing.

I jumped out of bed and ran into the hallway, pounding on the walls, shouting at the top of my lungs, *"Worm-eaters! Everybody wake up! There are worm-eaters outside!"*

But nobody was waking up.

I didn't know what else to do.

. . . and then I saw the fire alarm.

CHAPTER FIVE

I pushed through students outside, frantically searching for Dexter and Vic over the ringing bell of the fire alarm.

Everyone was angry about getting woken up, but I didn't care, because I was about to save the school again. What would this place do without me?

As the new headmaster shouted orders across the yard, the old headmaster finally made his first appearance.

Donald Kepler burst through the doors and scurried down the steps wearing nothing but his boxers and slippers, along with some kind of crazy lightbulb contraption on top of his head.

It was like something a mad scientist would wear to keep people from reading his thoughts.

I ran up to him. "Headmaster Kepler, I saw two worm-eaters out here, like, ten minutes ago! It was Dexter and Vic! They came outta the forest like this!"

I did my best worm-eater impression.

Kepler's eyes twitched. *"We must keep from making ripples,"* he said, panicked. And then he pulled me closer. *"What year is this? Has he escaped? He must be kept outside!"*

"What're you talking about? Did you hear what I said?"

The old man stepped backward slowly, studying me. *". . . Who are you?"*

Headmaster Archer came to Kepler's rescue, guiding him away from me and back toward the school.

Uh . . . What just happened?

Did Kepler forget who I was?

"Ha!" Vic laughed from behind me. "Nobody remembers losers!"

I spun around and bolted for the worm-eater. He freaked, putting his hands up to use his power, but I body-slammed him before he could.

Everyone was like, "*Ohhhhh!*" and then they started chanting, "*Fight! Fight! Fight!*"

I was a boy on a mission. If Vic was a worm-eater, his breath would smell like worms. All I needed was that bit of proof for everyone to have my back.

An army of Kepler students against two worm-eaters? Cake.

Vic and I scuffled as more students gathered around. My friends were right up front.

Vic stopped struggling. He pulled me closer and sloppily licked my face all over. *"Is this what you want?"*

I flinched, disgusted. *"Ah, gross, dude!"*

The spit on my face didn't smell like worms.

More like . . . candy?

The worm-eater crawled out from under me. I tried pulling him back by grabbing his hoodie, but he wriggled out of it, and I fell back onto the grass.

Coach Lindsay pushed through the crowd. "Knock it off, you two!"

I jumped up, pointing at Vic. *"Smell that boy's breath! I saw him walk out of the forest with Dexter! I bet his breath smells like worms!"*

Coach Lindsay was mortified, but not at Vic.

At me.

"That boy is a worm-eater!" I said again in case he didn't understand.

Vic's voice sliced through the air. *"Why are you calling me a boy?"*

I looked back at him, confused. "Because you're . . . you're a . . . wait, what?"

Penny gasped. "Oh, Ben, you beautiful idiot."

That was the first time I'd seen Vic without half his face hidden by hair and a hoodie—or, should I say, half *her* face hidden by hair and a hoodie.

Vic was a girl.

It was *way* more obvious without the hood.

Hushed whispers came from the crowd.

My world was rocked. "But . . . your name is Vic. Short for Victor."

"Short for *Victoria*, you *trash bag!*"

"But the *guyliner* . . ."

"It's just eyeliner when it's on a girl!"

"Time! Out!" Dexter said, making a T with his hands. "Did you think *Victoria* was a *dude* all last year?"

Everyone laughed.

Everyone except me and Vic.

She was holding back tears.

Not my best moment.

Everyone shuffled back to the dorms after the fire alarm was switched off. I stood next to Brock, wondering if running away to Mexico was easier than it sounded.

Penny, Noah, and Jordan sat next to me.

"I made a mistake," I said.

"Vic'll get over it," Penny said. "Someday. Careful, though, cuz she's super into Korean revenge movies. She'll become your closest friend for the next fifteen years, and then *BAM!* She cuts your brakes and watches you drive off a cliff."

"I swear I saw them, though. I saw Dexter and Vic out here," I said. "You guys believe me, right?"

They shrugged.

Noah spoke first. "I mean, it's three in the morning, and you have weird dreams anyway . . ."

"And Dexter and Vic weren't really acting like worm-eaters . . ." Penny added.

"And there's some half-eaten gummy worms in the grass over there . . ." Jordan said, pointing.

We all turned our heads.

Jordan was right. Chewed-up gummy worms were lying exactly where I saw Dexter and Vic standing from my window. They may not have been worm-eaters, but they *were* definitely outside after curfew, which brought back a sudden sense of panic in me.

Penny could tell. "Hey, relax, dude."

"I can't," I said, choking up. "I'm scared that something really, really bad is gonna happen this year. Like, *worse* than last year. That's how sequels work."

"Okay, so this isn't a movie," Penny said. "And you're not in a sequel."

"Nothing bad's gonna happen," Noah said. "You're just freaked out from last year."

I nodded reluctantly.

"But even if it does, we're all together now, side by side," Penny said. "We got your back."

That was all I needed to hear.

CHAPTER SIX

Four hours later, I was at breakfast, walking through a gauntlet of exhausted kids giving me the evil eye in the banquet hall.

Someone even beaned me in the head with a biscuit.

Who does that?

Noah waved to me from across the room. Penny and Jordan were with him. They had the whole table to themselves.

I sat across from Penny, but before I could dig into my food, a girl sat right next to me.

"Good morning, Benjamin!" she said with shiny eyes.

Her name was Millie Keegan. She was in the same grade as me, with the power of . . . something, I don't know.

I can't be expected to know *everyone's* power!

"You can call me Ben," I said.

Millie giggled. "Okay . . . *Ben*. Is anyone else sitting here?"

Noah shook his head.

"It's cool!" Millie said to a boy waiting patiently at the next table.

I recognized him, too—Arnold Solis, with the power to absorb other people's allergies.

MILLIE KEEGAN   ARNOLD SOLIS

Arnold grabbed his tray and squeezed in between Penny and Jordan.

"Hey, man," he said. "Big fan."

"We're the Braver Ravers!" Millie said. "Ben's fan club! We're the only two members, but I know I can grow it to a dozen by the end of the year."

"*Dude, you're a rock star,*" Noah whispered loud enough for everyone to hear.

"You're *Ben Braver!*" Arnold said. "The kid who defeated the first *actual* supervillain! You made history!"

Not gonna lie.

I liked the words coming out of Arnold's mouth.

"So he defeated a ten-story-tall monster version of himself," Penny said all nonchalant. "Whoop-di-spit."

Millie's face suddenly got serious. "I don't even care about *that*. I care that Ben *rescued* me from Abigail. She kidnapped me during the *second* week of school. She held me down as her vines wrapped around me. I was in my egg for *eight months*. How long were you in yours?"

Penny looked away. ". . . Like, an hour."

Millie continued, staring death at Penny. "If it wasn't for Ben, the *whole* school would have been in Abigail's army, *including* you."

"Sorry," Penny said quietly. "It was a bad joke."

"So what's your superpower?" Arnold asked me.

"My what?" I said.

"What power did you use to defeat Abigail?" Millie asked.

I forgot that everyone still thought I was hiding a superpower.

"Is it superstrength?" Arnold said.

"Maybe," I said. "Maybe not."

Again, not technically a lie.

Arnold glanced over his shoulder, then whispered, "I've been working on mine over the summer. So if the school's ever attacked again, I can help!"

"How?" Jordan asked. "By moochin' someone's peanut allergy?"

"I can steal powers now," Arnold said with a proud smile. "Let me show you!"

Arnold grabbed my hand, but I yanked it away.

"It won't hurt!" he said. "Your power comes back after a minute!"

I didn't care about it hurting.

I cared about being exposed as a phony.

Arnold and Millie waited eagerly for me to give my hand back. There was an awkward silence as Penny, Noah, and Jordan looked at one another.

Thankfully, Jordan saved me. "Do me!"

Arnold grabbed Jordan's sleeve, brought the invisible hand to his mouth, and took a huge chomp.

Jordan wailed, *"What's the matter with you—"* and then stopped suddenly.

Jordan's hand wasn't invisible anymore.

In fact, Jordan's whole body reappeared as Arnold's became invisible.

"Whaaaaat?" Noah said.

Penny was unimpressed. "He needs a haircut."

Jordan's hair was nearly shoulder length and curly. His fingers trembled as he stared at them with watery eyes.

Millie handed him a small mirror she pulled from her backpack.

". . . I look older!" he said with a humongous smile.

Everyone at the table realized he needed a moment. He was reuniting with someone he hadn't seen for a *very* long time.

"Told you I could do it," the freshly invisible Arnold said. "And I would've done the same thing to Abigail."

"You would've chickened out," Noah said.

"Yeah, wrong! I'd be all about it in the heat of battle. You'll see. Someday I'll fight a *real* villain, and positively *dominate* them. Those chumps won't even stand a chance!"

"But Noah has you beat," Jordan said. "He would've set that monster *ablaze, yo!*"

"Whatever!" Penny said. "Noah's nothing without his beef jerky. His kryptonite is a vegan diet!"

Noah puffed his chest out. "That's why *my* goal this year is to create fire *without* beef jerky. I'll be full-powered before the year's out!"

"Except this school's here to *prevent* that," Millie said.

"Does that seem right to you?" Arnold asked. "Can you imagine if *every* student here was full-powered, like me and Ben? Kepler kids could change the world, but they want us to be just like humans when we're *better* than that. We're *better* than humans."

A chill crawled up my spine.

Better than humans.

Arnold was sounding almost like Abigail.

"You make us sound like half-alien hybrids," Penny said. "I'm not into that."

"We're all thinking it," Arnold said as his face reappeared. "But I'm the only one with the guts to say it—*we could've been killed*. And it would've been Headmaster Kepler's fault."

"Lucky for us, Ben was there to save the day," Millie said.

Arnold smiled at me. "Heck yeah, he was."

Those two really liked me.

I wondered what they'd think if they knew I didn't have a power—if they knew I wasn't the big, bad superhero they thought I was.

Actually, scratch that.

I didn't want to know.

CHAPTER SEVEN

Later that day.

The library.

"Earth to Ben Braver," Penny whispered. "Come in, Ben Braver. Put that away and pay attention to me!"

Noah, Penny, and I were in the library digging through old yearbooks to figure out who Fifteen was. Jordan had passed on helping because he said it felt too much like homework.

Well, *Noah and Penny* were doing research. I was too busy sketching absolutely necessary stat cards for Dexter and Vic because bomb-diggity detectives take notes on everything, like strengths and weaknesses.

So I guess I could say I'm kinda like Batman.

I shut my sketchbook. "Sorry. Find anything yet?"

"No, but nothing's labeled," Penny said. "All we need is 1963. Fifteen's portrait should be in there *if* he went to school here."

I grabbed a random yearbook off the shelf, skimming photos until one caught my eye—it was of a girl sitting with the statue of Brock, eating lunch while reading a Garfield book.

She sat in the exact spot that I did when I ate lunch with Brock last year.

The girl looked incredibly sad, like one of those circus clowns, but without all the makeup, silly clothes, or props. So, really, nothing like a clown.

"Found it!" Penny said. "1963!"

Noah and I huddled over Penny.

She mumbled after every page until she found the first class's group photo. "Boo-yah! Yup . . . There's only fourteen students in this picture."

"That's the extra kid right there. Upper left corner," Noah said, comparing Penny's cell phone pic with the yearbook photo.

"He's kinda cute," Penny said.

"He's, like, seventy!" I said.

"Not in the picture, he's not!"

The photos were completely different, too. It wasn't that Fifteen was erased—it was that they took a second photo of the class without him. Students were in different spots, wearing different clothes.

Penny flipped through pages, scanning for another pic of Fifteen, but there weren't any.

Zero. Zip. Zilch.

No portrait.

Nothing in the club photos.

It was like he never existed, even though he totally did.

Penny opened to the double-page montage at the front of the book.

"There!" I said, jabbing my finger on one of the pictures. "That's Fifteen, right?"

Far in the background of the orientation-day photo was a boy wearing a plaid backpack. He was next to a woman with a Bride of Frankenstein–style beehive.

"He *was* there," Noah whispered.

Conspiracy confirmed.

The school was legit hiding a student from its own history. Something weird was def going on.

"That's gotta be his mom," Penny said, tapping the beehive lady.

"This would be easier if we knew his name," Noah said.

Penny snapped a picture of the picture with her phone. "This school documents everything, so there's gotta be extra photos from Year One. Miss Sweeney's in charge of Yearbook Club. I'll ask her for help."

"But don't tell her why," I warned.

"Duh," Penny said. "I have a history report about one of the Seven Keys anyway. I'll tell her it's for that."

DEXTER DUNN

SUPERPOWER: ICE CONJURER
POWER LEVEL: ☆ ☆ ☆ ☆
WEAKNESS: FIRE AND HE'S SLOW (BOTH MENTALLY AND PHYSICALLY)

DEXTER IS LIKE A BIG, DUMB APE - MOSTLY HARMLESS IF YOU STAY AWAY FROM HIM, BUT ABLE TO RIP YOU TO SHREDS IF HE LOSES HIS TEMPER.

EASILY ONE OF THE MORE POWERFUL AND DANGEROUS STUDENTS AT KEPLER ACADEMY.

VICTORIA VICARS

SUPERPOWER: LEVITATION
POWER LEVEL: ☆ ☆
WEAKNESS: EASILY DISTRACTED

VICTORIA IS DEFINITELY NOT A BOY.

HER POWER OF LEVITATION INCLUDES THE ABILITY TO FLY BY LEVITATING HERSELF. SHE CAN LEVITATE SMALL OBJECTS LIKE BASEBALLS OR EVEN PEOPLE, BUT I'VE NEVER SEEN HER LIFT ANYTHING HEAVIER, LIKE A CAR.

BEN BRAVER

SUPERPOWER: NONE
POWER LEVEL: NONE
WEAKNESS: I'M HUMAN

GOOD LOOKS AND GREAT HAIR DON'T MEAN ANYTHING WHEN YOU'RE UP AGAINST SOMEONE WITH A SUPERPOWER.

BUT, FOR REAL, I'M ONE GOOD-LOOKIN' KID.

CHAPTER EIGHT

In the meantime, I turned back to my other ongoing investigation: discovering why Dexter and Vic had been out in the forest the night we arrived at the academy. I spied on them all week, but I still had nothing.

My only observation was how tired they were all the time, but nobody would bust them for that.

The sky was crystal clear as Penny and I headed to Brock's statue for lunch.

"You notice how all the adults are acting weird this year?" I asked. "Like, they're super cheerful *all* the time."

"They're acting like last year didn't happen," Penny said. "They think students are freaked out, so they're pretending everything is all sunshine and rainbows."

"Most kids don't seem freaked out, though."

"Then maybe they're pretending to make themselves feel better."

"Oh . . . That's wicked deep."

As we walked up, we saw Coach sitting by Brock with a crumpled cupcake wrapper in his hand. Two untouched cupcakes were beside him, one with a burned-down candle.

"He would've been forty-four today," Coach said. "I always have a cupcake with him on his birthday."

He was talking about Brock.

Obvi.

"You gonna eat those two extra cupcakes?" I asked, eyeballing the sweet treats.

"Go ahead." Coach smiled. "They shouldn't go to waste."

Penny held out her hand as I grabbed both cupcakes and set them on my lap.

"Oh, cool, they're *both* for you," Penny said sarcastically. "Enjoy *both* of your cupcakes, Scrooge."

I made a "whatever" face before handing one over.

"Did you know him?" I asked.

"I didn't," Coach said. "But I knew his sister."

"He had a sister?"

Coach nodded. "Angel Blackwood. She came here in

1994, a year after my twin sister, Olivia, and I started. Three years before that was when Brock turned to stone. Angel would eat lunch with this statue every day, a lot like you did last year, Ben."

"Oh, I saw a picture of her!" I said. I looked down at my cupcake. "She looked like the saddest girl in the world."

"Probably cuz she was eating lunch with the stone-dead body of her brother," Penny said. "That's dark. Like, *dark* dark. Like, *mess-you-up* dark."

"What if Brock's not dead?" I asked, hopeful.

"If he's not, then I hope he's asleep," Penny said. "Or else he's trapped in a nightmare—turned to stone but able to see and hear everything?"

"That'd be the worst," I said.

"Nah," Coach said, standing. "Nobody really knows what happens when you die, but there's worse in life."

"Worse than turning yourself into a statue?" I asked.

"I believe the worst thing to happen when you die would be meeting the person you *could've* become."

"How's that worse?"

Penny thought for a moment. "Hmm, how can I put this into nerdspeak? Okay, Clark Kent is Superman, right?"

"Right," I said.

"So what if Clark Kent didn't know he could be Superman? And he was just a boring farmer until he died of old age. And he *never* became Superman."

"That'd be lamest of lames . . ."

"Right, but it'd be *lamer* if Superman showed up right before Clark Kent died and was, like, 'Hey, dude, you could'a been me, but now you're dead. LOL. Too bad, so sad. Hashtag, sorry not sorry.'"

"Superman's a jerk in your lesson," I said.

Penny took a bite of her cupcake. "He sure is."

Coach chuckled. "Angel Blackwood's power was similar to yours, actually, Penny, if not identical."

"Descendants can have the same powers?" I asked.

"It's rare, but it happens," Coach said. "Usually it happens between siblings. My twin sister and I both had superstrength."

FYI—Coach's sister died a long time ago.

"Angel controlled animals with music," Coach continued, "but she didn't use a ukulele. She used her voice. She sang, and animals listened."

"Your power probably works like hers did," Coach said. "We all have some kind of energy inside us, keeping us alive. A soul, a spirit, whatever. Angel could *manipulate* her energy—her spirit—and use it as a weapon by projecting rays of pure energy. But a side effect of her power was that she could transfer a small part of it into another living being, basically turning them into a mind-controlled slave. It's what you do to mice."

"Are you saying I'll be able to shoot energy blasts someday?" Penny whispered excitedly.

"The academy would frown upon that," Coach said with a smirk. "I'm saying that controlling mice *isn't* your real power."

A red flag suddenly snapped in my head. "Abigail said she was working with someone who could mind-control people! What if Angel is who she was talking about?"

"Not possible. Angel died in 2008."

"How do you know she didn't fake her own death?"

"Because my *sister* died with her."

"Ohhh . . . kay, then," I said, feeling stupid. "Sorry."

Coach continued. "Angel always had a cupcake with Brock on his birthday even after she graduated. She would make a trip to the school just for that. Sometimes my sister would go along, too. One night, Angel and Olivia were at the end of their trip. Angel drove all day, fell asleep at the wheel, and veered off a bridge close to here." Coach took a slow, deep breath. "Her car exploded when it hit the ground."

Coach was quiet for a moment.

It was one of those sad, awkward moments you always read about but never experience.

"Throw those wrappers away when you're done, okay?" he said, leaving Penny and me alone with the statue.

We spent the rest of lunch eating in silence.

NOAH NICHOLS

SUPERPOWER: FIRE CONJURER
POWER LEVEL: ✰ ✰✰✰
WEAKNESS: WATER, AND LACK OF BEEF JERKY

NOAH CAN BREATHE FIRE, CONJURE FIRE FROM
HIS HANDS, AND FLY BY SHOOTING FIRE FROM
HIS FEET, BUT ONLY WHEN HE EATS BEEF JERKY,
WHICH HE KEEPS IN HIS POCKET AT ALL TIMES
MAKING HIM SMELL LIKE SMOKED TURKEY LEGS
FROM THE CARNIVAL. WITHOUT HIS JERKY, HE'S
NOTHING.

PENNY ~~BRAVER~~ PLUM

SUPERPOWER: MOUSE CONTROL
POWER LEVEL: ✰
WEAKNESS: HER UKULELE

PENNY CONTROLS MICE WITH HER UKE, BUT
I THINK SHE'LL BE ABLE TO CONTROL MORE
SOMEDAY - MAYBE EVEN PEOPLE.

PENNY NEEDS HER UKE TO BRING HER POWER OUT.
TAKE AWAY HER UKE: TAKE AWAY HER POWER.

ANOTHER STRENGTH IS SHE'S **SOOOO** PRETTY.

JORDAN SOMETHING

SUPERPOWER: INVISIBILITY
POWER LEVEL: ✰
WEAKNESS: BABY POWDER AND GIRLS

JORDAN BECAME FULLY INVISIBLE LAST YEAR,
BUT CAN'T SWITCH THAT POWER OFF. HE'S
INVISIBLE 24/7 WITH NO SIGNS OF EVER
BECOMING VISIBLE AGAIN, BUT I'M NOT SURE IF
HE'S EVER TRIED.

JORDAN WOULD MAKE THE PERFECT SPY, BUT
HE'D HAVE TO BE NAKED THE WHOLE TIME.

CHAPTER NINE

5:55 p.m.

Late September.

Watching Dexter had gotten me nowhere, but I knew something sinister was *definitely* goin' down. So it was time to start following him.

Earlier that day, Millie tipped me off on some chatter she'd overheard about kids going with Dexter after dark. Real hush-hush stuff.

It was the opportunity I'd been waiting for.

The plan was simple—use Penny's cell phone as a tracking device to follow him.

Jordan and I would wait in our dorm while Noah and Penny would wait in the lobby. Once Dexter exited the elevator for dinner, Penny would call us using the coffee shop phone—our signal to sneak into Dexter's room and plant *her* phone in his backpack. Then we'd use the Phone Finder app on Penny's laptop to track him.

Pretty brilliant, right?

It would've worked perfectly except dinner was almost over, and Dexter was still in his room.

I called the coffee shop from Penny's cell.

"Cool Beanz, how can I help you?"

"Is Penny Plum there?"

"Penny? No, sorry, bud, you got the wrong number."

"She's one of your customers."

"You called to talk to a customer? This line is for business—" The phone dropped. *"Hey! Let go—get off the counter!"*

There was muffled shouting, then Penny's voice spoke loud and clear. *"Heeeey."*

"Where's Dexter?"

"I don't know. He hasn't come out of the elevator yet."

"Is he just sitting in his dorm or something?"

"Uh, I don't know?" She paused. "Oh . . . oh, wait.

There he is! I see him! Uhhhh-oh. He's getting *into* the elevator. I think he was already at dinner!"

"For real?"

"Yeeeeah," Penny said. "We must've missed him the first time. Bummer. You should go, 'kay? Bye!"

"Flippin' eggs!" I said, ending the call.

With Dexter on the elevator, we had only a minute to plant the phone.

It was go-time.

Jordan and I raced to Dexter's dorm. Jordan beat me to the door so he could pick the lock, but the thing wasn't even locked!

I pushed past Jordan to get into Dexter's dorm.

The air was thick and wet and smelly. It was like getting punched in the face with a fart.

Jordan shut the door and kept watch through the peephole while I searched for the backpack.

"Hurry up," Jordan said.

"I can't find it!" I said, tearing through the closet.

"Check the bathroom!"

I pinched my nose and poked my head inside. "Why would he keep it in—oh, there it is."

Dexter's backpack hung from the showerhead he probably never used.

Instead of schoolbooks, I found purple and yellow clothing rolled up inside. After putting Penny's phone under the fabric, I went back to Jordan.

"The phone's planted. Let's book!" I said.

Jordan reached for the door handle, but it turned before he touched it.

Dexter was about to come in.

I panicked and latched the dead bolt.

"Good thinking," Jordan whispered. "He'll never suspect the door *locking itself*."

"*Hey, who's in there?*" Dexter shouted from outside. "*Who's in my room?*"

Jordan and I were trapped.

There were only two ways out of that mess. Battle the troll at the door . . . or risk our lives out the window.

I think we made the right choice. . . .

CHAPTER TEN

Twenty minutes later.

"**Y**ou know, looking back, this might've been the wrong choice," I said.

"Ya think?" Jordan said.

We were standing on a ledge three stories off the ground.

The easy part was inching back to our window four rooms away. The hard part was trying to unlock the window from the outside. They're not really designed to do that.

Penny and Noah hadn't returned from the lobby yet, so we'd been stuck outside for twenty minutes.

And it was starting to rain.

Finally, my front door opened. Penny and Noah raced over and slid the window open.

"Hey, guys," Penny said. "Whatcha dooooin'?"

"Move!" Jordan said, knocking me off balance as he fell through the window like a flopping fish.

He went into the room.

I went over the ledge.

Noah caught me by my ankle. Penny grabbed his waist, and Jordan grabbed hers, making a chain of kids trying to save my life.

I hung upside down far enough that I dangled outside the window of the dorm beneath mine.

Millie was inside, at the far end of the room. Mae, her roommate, was right next to their open window, reading a book. Both faced away from me.

Last year, Mae caught me taking a sample of her sweat during my worm-eater investigation, but before I could explain myself, she decked me with a right hook.

I don't blame her. I looked like a creeper collecting her sweat. That's *almost* as bad as looking like a creeper peeking through her window.

No sudden movements.

No loud noises.

Just pull myself up and everything will be okay.

Noah's voice blared from above. *"Ben! Ben, hang on, Ben! We're trying to pull you up, Ben, but you're super heavy!"*

I waved back and forth, trying to get Noah's attention. "Stop shouting my name!" I hissed.

"Ben, what? Whaaaat, Ben? Why are you whispering? Arrrre youuu okaaay, Ben?"

I pushed my finger against my lips to tell my friend to shut his stupid mouth, but it wasn't working.

I think he knew exactly what he was doing.

"Benjamin Braver, just hang on! We're pulling you up, Ben Braver from room 310!" Noah howled.

Noah tugged on my ankle. I thought we might be making progress when I went up an inch, but then my jeans ripped, and I shot back down half a foot.

"No!" I shouted.

Millie turned around, gawking at me. Mae glanced up at Millie, confused.

I watched Mae's head turn ever so slowly.

Her eyes met mine.

"Hi!" I said. "So this is *not* what it looks like."

She screamed as she threw her book at me.

I flinched. My jeans tore in two.

And everything went black.

I woke up wearing a tuxedo in a room at the Heartbreak Hotel in outer space.

Stars twinkled outside the window as lights from a floating city glinted from miles away.

"Are you okay?" a woman asked from the bathroom.

My wife.

I'd know her voice anywhere.

"I think so," I said. "I had that weird dream again. . . ."

"The one where you fall off a school building?"

Was that the dream?

"Maybe?" I said. "I had to break into someone's room . . . crawl out the window, and . . . Millie was there . . . ?"

"*Who's Millie?*" My wife stepped out of the bathroom, still fixing an earring to the side of her head, which was weird because she had no ears.

She was a peanut butter cup.

We were on our honeymoon *on* the moon as happy newlyweds.

At least until that moment.

My wife marched over, glaring at me the whole way. "How dare you think she's prettier than me!"

"I never said that!"

"That's *exactly* what you said when you didn't say anything at all! *Who. Is. Millie?*"

"She's just a *friend* from school! I-I think I saw her before I woke up!" I said, terrified because an angry, mutant peanut butter cup was *horrifying*.

Why did I marry that thing?

My wife stopped by the bed and smiled gently. "Ah . . . okay. I understand now . . ." she said, reaching under her pillow.

I sighed. "Oh, good, because I thought—"

The peanut butter cup spun around, igniting a light-saber and pointing it directly at my face. "I understand that my cover's been blown. Tell me where the Reaper is and *maybe* I'll let you live."

Betrayed by my own wife!

On our honeymoon!

"The Reaper? I don't know what you're talking about!" I said.

"I'm talking about the supervillain who killed the world! We know you're hiding him somewhere on earth! Tell me where he is or *you* die!"

The lightsaber buzzed as she drew closer to me.

"He isn't real! Please don't do this! Put the lightsaber down, and let's talk like civilized tweens!"

Did I just call myself a tween?

Ew.

My wife raised the glowing laser sword high above her head and looked at me with sadness in her eyes. *"Je t'aimerai pour toujours. Au revoir, mon amour."*

"Wait, what? I don't speak Spanish!"

The ceiling suddenly crumbled above us, and down came a squadron of moon soldiers pinning my wife to the ground.

I was heartbroken.

She was an intergalactic assassin . . . but I *loved* her.

A girl slid down a rope and landed in front of me.

It was Millie.

I opened my eyes, staring up at my friends. Millie was there, too. I was back at the academy. I must've zonked out when I fell from my window.

Millie had one hand on my forehead and the other on my chest.

"He's fine," Penny said, annoyed. "You can stop touching him now."

"How'd you do that?" I asked.

"That's my power," Millie said with a soft smile. "I can visit other people's dreams."

Jordan sat up straight. "So that was actually *you* visiting me in my dream last night?"

Millie made a face. "Uh . . . no. *That* wasn't me."

"*Daaang!*" Penny said, slapping Jordan's back. "*How super awkward for you!*"

"Are you all right?" Noah asked. "I totally would've flown out the window to catch you, but, y'know . . . no beef jerky. You're lucky these bushes were here to break your fall."

"Right." I groaned. "*Lucky.*"

"Did you do it?" Penny asked. "Did you plant my phone?"

"Yup," I said. "Now all we have to do is wait."

CHAPTER ELEVEN

11 p.m.

My dorm.

Five hours of waiting.
Nothing.

To stay awake, my friends started killing time by making fun of my not having a power, but subtly, since Millie had joined our stakeout, and she didn't know I was powerless.

"But Bruce Wayne and Tony Stark are rich," Noah said. "You're not a billionaire."

"Yet," I said.

"Why would you need to be a billionaire?" Millie asked.

I scrambled for an answer, but Penny saved me.

"Why *wouldn't* he wanna be a billionaire?" Penny said.

Millie nodded with an "*Mmm*" sound. That answer was good enough.

"Becoming a billionaire is easy," I said. "All it takes is a couple of good inventions to get there."

Noah laughed. "Name *one* good thing you've ever invented."

"The tooth-plunger!" I said.

Millie shuddered. "Is that something that sucks your teeth out?"

"Ew, no!" I said. "It's a combination toothbrush-plunger! It's a two-in-one thing!"

"*Whaaaaaat?*" Jordan said. "That's *brilliant*! I wanna get in on the ground floor of that, okay? Hello, *Shark Tank*? One billion dollars, please!"

"*Nerds of a feather,*" Penny whispered.

She refreshed the Phone Finder app for the millionth time. "Stakeouts always sound more fun than they are. Dexter's still just sitting there."

"We need to wait a little longer," I said.

"But boredom is the worst way to die!" Penny whined.

"What if he leaves at three in the morning? That's when I saw him last time."

Penny shut her laptop. "I'm *not* staying up that late!"

"You can't give up! What if he leaves *right* now?" I whined.

"We've got *class* in the morning, duuude," Penny whined right back.

"It's not *all* night," I said, taking Penny's computer. "Just *half* the night. Take a nap or something. I'll keep watch."

I looked at the map on the screen, but I wasn't sure what to do. An overhead shot of the school showed a green dot for Penny's laptop, but I didn't see the dot for her phone—the one in Dexter's backpack.

"How do I work this?" I asked. "What's Dexter's dot look like?"

Penny yawned, stretching out on my bed. "It's the red blip right next to the green blip."

I refreshed the screen, and suddenly Dexter's dot pinged. Both dots were there, but they weren't next to each other. The green one was in my dorm, but the red one was in downtown Lost Nation.

"It says he's in the city," I said.

Penny grumbled as she pried her eyes open to see the screen. She blinked. And then she blinked again. "The app's confused. It glitches when the signal gets lost."

"So did he leave?" Millie asked.

"No. It means he found my phone and turned it off," Penny explained, hopping up. "I'm gonna get it back."

"Wait, you can't just barge in there!" I said as everyone followed Penny down the hall.

"Why not?" Penny said.

"Because of our plan!"

"Our plan was to follow him wherever he went and then steal my phone back. It wasn't to let him *keep* my phone if he found it."

"But you're just gonna walk in and grab it? Shouldn't we sneak in?"

Penny stopped at Dexter's door.

"Sneak in?" she said. "Why? He already caught us. Have you not been paying attention? That thing's worth more than Jordan Janke's life, so I need to get it back before Dexter gets it greasy with his fingers."

"Wait, who's Jordan Janke?" I asked before I realized the big-time mistake I just made.

All eyes were on me.

I laughed nervously. "I just, um . . . Oh, you mean Jordan *Janke*! I thought you said Jordan *Stanky*, and I was like, *who is that?*"

"You didn't know my last name?" Jordan said.

"I did! Not. The full last name. Was what I didn't. I just, I forgot it. Kind of. I'm sorry."

Clearly, my brain had hit a wall.

"I hate you," Jordan said.

Penny pushed Dexter's door open, and the five of us ran inside, ready for the Battle for Penny's Phone.

But he wasn't anywhere in there.

Suddenly a car horn honked from the closet.

We looked at one another because it definitely wasn't a normal "closet" kind of sound.

Millie went in first. "What if that red blip was right? What if Dexter *did* go into the city?"

My heart started pounding. The investigation was my idea, but I was having second thoughts.

We huddled together inside the closet. The sound of squealing tires came from behind a hanging bedsheet that fluttered.

Millie pulled the sheet aside.

Behind it, propped open by a makeshift ring of coat hangers, was a portal to the Kepler garage.

Dexter *was* in Lost Nation.

My act 2 started with a single step through Joel's portal into the Kepler garage in Lost Nation.

The garage was dark.

"Where is everyone?" Penny asked.

"We should go back," I said.

"This whole thing was *your* idea," Penny snapped.

"That doesn't make it a *good* one!"

"Aw, *somebody's* scared," Jordan said.

Millie looked at me like a worried pup.

"I'm not *scared*," I said. "I'm just—we don't know what we're gonna find, and, like, I don't want *Millie* to get hurt."

"I'll be fine," Millie said. "As long as you're here, we're all safe."

Penny melted. "Yes, Ben, we'll all be okay as long as you're the wind beneath our wings."

Millie nodded, not getting that the joke was on her.

We snuck out to the alley, wet from the rain. A trail of grimy footprints led to the run-down warehouse next door, where we could hear kids talking and laughing.

We didn't want to barge right through the front door, so we quickly climbed up a rusty fire escape and slipped in through an open window.

Once inside, I realized the warehouse wasn't a warehouse at all, but an abandoned factory that looked like a multiplayer map from *Call of Duty*. Years of dust covered old, rusted machinery that surrounded the empty center of the dark building.

In that empty center was a circle of kids wearing brightly colored costumes. Standing before them was Dexter, decked out in the purple and yellow fabric I had seen in his backpack earlier.

"We're at the start of another good week," Dexter said. "We're still under the radar, but that ain't hard when teachers are too busy babysitting rowdy kids now that Old Man Kepler's lost his marbles."

Everyone laughed.

"Just remember, these aren't fights. This is *battle* training. Practicing. Preparing. A real-life supervillain attacked us last year, and we were all helpless little babies, but we *won't* be caught with our pants down again."

"Good thing Ben Braver was there to save us," someone said. "Will he be invited, too?"

Dexter ground his teeth. "That bo-jo got lucky, and *no*, he's *not* invited. True descendants of the Seven Keys only."

It wasn't like I was dying to join Dexter's party, but getting singled out was still a bummer.

"This is *top secret*," Dexter said. "And *Braver* almost *wrecked* it when he caught Vic and me comin' out of the forest after tryin' to find a place to do this."

Vic spoke up from the circle. "Best thing to happen to us. This old building is *way* cooler than the forest. And it's farther away from all the teachers."

"Welcome to the most epic secret tournament the world has ever *not* seen," Dexter said. "*Welcome to the Power Battle.*"

Everyone cheered.

Some had capes. Some even had masks.

I understood exactly what was happening.

They were training to be superheroes.

Dexter's voice boomed. "For our first match of the night—Balloon Boy versus Death Bunny!"

If I wanted to get a closer look, I'd have to crawl out on one of the catwalks, but first I needed a disguise. Luckily, I had a secret mask in case of emergencies.

A boy and a girl took the center of the circle and powered up. The boy stuck his thumb into his mouth and blew like he was blowing up a balloon. He huffed and puffed until his fist was the size of a beach ball.

"Go easy, dude!" Vic warned him. "You don't wanna make yourself explode!"

The girl fell onto her hands and knees, transforming in front of everyone. Her clothes ripped off, and white fur replaced the skin all over her body as she grew into a buffalo-size bunny with red eyes and sharp teeth.

"I wanna pet that!" Penny gasped.

"I hope she's got extra clothes," Millie said.

Death Bunny's roar shook the windows as she charged at Balloon Boy.

He jumped out of the way and then swung his balloon fist into the side of Death Bunny's face. But the adorable beast wasn't even fazed.

She head-butted Balloon Boy, who went flying through the wall of students behind him.

Death Bunny pounded across the factory at ramming speed.

I couldn't believe how hard-core the battle was. Neither one of them was holding back.

Balloon Boy flipped onto his feet, blew his fist even bigger, and swung his arm in circles like he was winding up a punch.

He nailed the furry white monster with an uppercut that sent her through the air, on a crash course for the catwalk I was hiding on.

Of course.

Everyone looked up just as Death Bunny tore through the catwalk, sending the whole thing falling to the center of their circle.

Kids dove out of the way as I hurtled face-first toward the ground.

Vic stopped me midair before I kissed the concrete. She flipped me right side up and kept me floating with my feet just above the ground.

Whispers came from the crowd.

"Where'd Ben Braver come from?"

"What's Ben Braver doing here?"

They said it just like that, too.

Not just Ben, but Ben *Braver*.

My whole name.

Dexter met me face-to-underwear-covered-face.

"You forget how undies work?" he asked.

"No. It's my disguise."

"And you just happened to have an extra pair of underwear with you?"

I thought very carefully before answering that question. ". . . Yes," I said. "Yes, I did."

"You're like a fly that won't buzz off!" Dexter said.

"It's hard for a fly to buzz off when there's a steaming pile of turd in front of him!" I said, my mouth talking before my brain gave it permission.

Dexter fumed, but Vic put her hand on his shoulder.

"Dude," she said. "He's *in* the circle."

A smile curled on Dexter's face. "For our second match of the night . . ."

ME VERSUS BEN DOVER.

CHAPTER THIRTEEN

Dexter and I faced each other across the small circle as Vic levitated the broken catwalk out of the way.

Penny, Noah, and Millie had joined the group and were right behind me, but Jordan was nowhere to be seen, which meant he either ducked out or was still around somewhere—just naked and hiding.

Speaking of naked, Death Bunny *did, in fact,* have an extra outfit she had changed into after her match.

I should've walked away, but the small crowd was chanting, "*Ben Bra-ver! Ben Bra-ver! Ben Bra-ver!*"

Millie started the chant, but it still counts.

"What're you gonna do?" Noah asked. "Dexter's not gonna go easy on you."

"Just run," Penny said. "Nobody will judge you. Not to your face, at least."

If I tried to battle Dexter, then the crowd would find out fast that I didn't have a power. But if I let him kill me right away, then my secret would die with me.

Choices, choices.

Millie scowled. "Ben defeated a giant monster last year. Dexter's a gnat compared with that!"

Oh, right.

Millie didn't know I was powerless.

"*Yeah*, you guys," I said. "Dexter's just a gnat. A scary, man-size, superpowered gnat."

"You're gonna die," Penny said as Vic announced the match.

Dexter and I met at the center of the circle. "Don't worry, dude," I said, faking confidence. Maybe I could mess with his head. "I'll go easy on ya."

Dexter smirked. "All I need to worry about is where to hide your body when this is over."

Whoooa . . . that got dark fast.

"Battle!" Vic shouted.

Dexter threw his hands to his sides, palms up, and his entire body burst with steam. His skin crystallized as his eyes became empty sockets.

I just stood there.

A thin sheet of ice formed at Dexter's feet as the air around him froze into sparkling particles of ice and snowflakes and Disney magic.

And I just kept standing there.

Dexter fired ice across the ring like he was in *Super Smash Bros.* I dodged it, but barely. The ice clipped my shoulder and frost-burned me as I fell to the ground.

"Too easy," Dexter said.

I tried scooting back, but a path of ice cut across the

floor from Dexter's foot to mine, crawling up my leg and freezing me in place.

"Get up, Ben!" Millie shouted.

Noah pulled out a stick of beef jerky, ready to jump in to save me, but it never came to that.

Dexter's foot slipped wildly out from under him, and he totally ate it, ice-skater–style. He tried to get up, but his body started spinning circles on the icy floor.

Penny's and Noah's jaws dropped.

Millie cheered.

The ice around my foot shattered, and I rolled to my feet, totally confused.

Then a familiar voice whispered in my ear. "Wave your arms around like you have a power. I got this."

Jordan was fully invisible and battling for me!

Which also meant he was fully naked.

Yuck.

Dexter came at me like a lunatic in a blizzard of snow. I threw out kung fu moves that Bruce Lee taught me himself. Through clips on YouTube.

"Foot sweep!" I shouted, hoping Jordan would follow my lead.

He totally did.

Dexter tripped, landing on his face.

"*Did you see that?*" someone from the circle said. "*He just used his brain to knock that kid down!*"

I sliced my hand through the air. "Throat punch!"

Dexter grabbed his throat and fell to his knees.

Millie gave me a high five when I turned to gloat.

"And now for my finishing move," I said, curling my fingers.

Dexter's face turned red as his underwear was magically pulled out of the back of his pants. Jordan wedgied him so hard that he lifted Dexter off the ground for a second.

Dexter shook himself free, grabbed his butt cheeks, and ran out of the factory crying.

The crowd cheered.

Penny and Noah couldn't stop laughing.

Millie nearly knocked me down with a hug.

I was the champion.

The winner of the battle.

And I did absolutely nothing to deserve it.

CHAPTER FOURTEEN

The Power Battle was over.

A few other battles followed, but only one was epic.

Mine.

Eventually the rest of the kids went back to the school, leaving me, Penny, and Noah alone in the abandoned factory.

I stood in the center of the cavernous space, imagining how awesome I must've looked to everyone else.

"All right, dude, it's, like, one in the morning. Time to make like a baby and head out." Penny yawned, pushing her phone into her pocket. She'd snuck it out of Dexter's bag during my match with him.

Noah struggled to stay awake, bobbing his head every few seconds. "Pillows . . . blankets . . . please . . ."

"Hang on," I said. "Still basking."

Penny rolled her eyes. "Fine, then we're leaving without you."

Noah trailed behind Penny as they walked into the

alley back to the portal in the Kepler garage, leaving me by myself in the dark.

"No, wait up, guys! I'm done basking!" I shouted, running to catch up.

I got outside just in time to see the door to the Kepler garage slam shut.

I dashed toward the door handle, but my fingers barely grazed it before I was yanked into the air.

Dexter and Vic stepped out from the shadows.

"All this trouble for an autograph?" I said. "All you had to do was ask, but it'll cost you five bucks."

Vic pinched the air in front of her.

The skin around my neck tightened, and my throat closed as she lifted me higher off the ground.

I think she was still upset at the whole *thinking-she-was-a-boy-for-a-year* thing.

"*Wait, wait, stop!*" I wheezed.

Vic let up a little. "What?"

"*You can have my autograph for free!*"

"You're a poser!" Dexter said. "I don't have proof, but I know you cheated. *Something* pushed me around in there. *Someone* pushed me. Having an invisible buddy is pretty convenient, ain't it?"

Vic scowled as she spread her fingers open.

My arms stretched out as I dangled helplessly. The skin on my shoulders burned, and my bones felt like they were gonna snap at any second.

"*Stop!*" I said.

At that moment, a Vespa engine revved, and a headlight flipped on from the street behind Dexter and Vic.

Vic's grip loosened. "What the . . ."

The rider stepped off the scooter, black leather pants and jacket shining, her face hidden by her helmet.

It was the same woman I'd seen outside the academy on the first night. The Vespa ninja!

The air around Dexter sizzled as he powered up, looking even stronger than he did in the Power Battle. His skin became jagged shards of ice. Even his face changed into something monstrous.

Dexter's voice sounded cold. "You should get back on your bike and get outta here, lady."

The biker walked slowly toward us, unfazed by Dexter's transformation into an ice monster.

"*Did you hear me?*" Dexter's voice cracked.

"Dude, she's not stopping," Vic said nervously.

"Fine. Then she asked for it."

The air swirled around Dexter's forearm as he aimed at the biker. Several chunks of ice launched toward her like torpedoes.

The icicles cracked the woman's visor. She fell back, landing on her butt.

"Throw him," Dexter commanded.

"What?" Vic said.

"Throw Ben at her!"

FYI: I was *against* that idea.

Vic flicked her fingers, and I went flying through the alley.

The woman jumped to her feet just in time for me to crash into her, and we both rolled on the dirty, wet pavement.

It hurt.

Like, *a lot.*

I tried to stand, but my head spun in circles. The alley tipped sideways as I swayed back and forth with my hands out like an old man wearing a blindfold.

What?

Dexter and Vic were gone.

They would've closed Joel's portal behind them, for sure.

I was alone and stranded in Lost Nation, trying to get away from a Vespa ninja, who was back on her feet and reaching for me.

I swatted her hand away. "Don't touch me!" I shouted, stumbling back toward the Kepler garage.

A muffled voice came from under her cracked

helmet. I couldn't tell exactly what she said, but it *sounded* like . . .

"Did you just . . ." I said, confused. "Did you just say my name?"

She pried the helmet off her head.

Blond hair fell over her face as she shook it loose. She swung her head back, flipping the hair over her shoulder.

CHAPTER FIFTEEN

Thirty minutes later, I was sitting in Campion's Diner, digging into a slice of peanut butter cup pie.

Life's weird like that.

The biker sat across from me.

Her name was Jennifer Jenkins, and she worked

for the academy, secretly scoping out the streets of Lost Nation to make sure people didn't stumble upon the school.

She was bright-eyed and all smiles. Hardly the scary Vespa ninja I thought she was.

But just so you don't think I'd jump on the back of *any* stranger's scooter, she let me call Coach Lindsay, who backed her up—he told me she worked for him on the academy's security team.

JENNIFER JENKINS

Jennifer must be one of the "people" everyone keeps talking about when they say "they have people for that."

She also never mentioned the Power Battle to Coach. All she said was that I snuck into the city, which maybe was pretty common with Kepler students? Probably more so with the older ones.

I thought Coach would be furious, but since I was safe with Jennifer, he said he'd let me off the hook this time. I mean, he *did* threaten that he wouldn't be as forgiving if it happened again. But that was basically the same as being let off the hook, which was fantastically cool of him—*and* I got to have a slice of pie.

Okay, I got to have *three* slices.

Don't judge me.

The waitress brought me a glass of milk.

"Has Elvis left the building yet?" I asked.

"What?" the waitress asked, annoyed.

"Elvis? A couple of weeks ago, I saw a kid . . . wearing an Elvis Presley mask . . . outside. Nevermind."

She looked at Jennifer, like, *"What's he talkin' about?"*

Jennifer shrugged.

The waitress left, and I chugged my milk.

"Are you gonna tell Headmaster Archer about the Power Battle?" I asked.

"No," Jennifer said. "It's just kids being kids. Just keep 'em low-key and we're good. We did the same thing when I was in school. Heck, some adults still do it today to blow off steam."

I poked at my pie with my fork. "Maybe that's what Abigail needed last year."

"Abigail needed more than that. That woman was a lunatic." Jennifer sighed. "She was always the nicest lady, too."

"I think she saw something she wasn't supposed to see," I said.

A suspicious smile stretched across Jennifer's face. ". . . What do you know?"

"I know she found Kepler's secret cave. Something in there made her snap, but I don't know what."

"That old man has a secret cave?"

"*Had* one," I said. "Pretty sure it caved in when that monster went full Godzilla mode, but it was packed with crazy. Newspaper articles about things that never happened."

To be honest, it felt good to say these things to an adult who understood.

"Don't be so quick to say those things never happened. With the snap of his finger, Donald Kepler can have your mind wiped. He has people for that."

". . . Are *you* one of those people?"

Jennifer shook her head. "Oh no. *Those* people—you'd *know* those people if you saw them."

"So what's *your* power?"

She hesitated, then put her hands up. She was still wearing her gloves. "My skin is ultrasensitive to oxygen. If anything more than my face is exposed, I start to feel woozy."

"Man, some powers *aren't* cool, huh?"

Jennifer sighed. "Nope."

"Anyway," I said. "Those things in the articles were too big to wipe from history—end-of-the-world big.

Blown-up cities. Millions dead. Real-life superheroes." I took a bite of pie and continued. "I don't know. I was on the roof when Abigail attacked. She told Kepler that she knew his secret. Something in that cave freaked her out enough to make her a bad guy."

"Well, we're lucky you were up there. You saved the day with your secret power."

I stared at my pie.

The only people who knew I was powerless were my best friends, Donald Kepler, and Professor Duncan.

Not even my parents knew.

". . . I don't actually have a power."

I'm not sure why I confessed.

Maybe I just wanted someone else to know.

Maybe Jennifer kinda felt like a big sister I never had.

Maybe I'm just a moron.

Jennifer straightened up. "How'd you beat that giant monster then?"

"It was only giant because it had one of Professor Duncan's discs attached to it. I just ripped off the disc."

"*Brilliant*," Jennifer whispered. "You know, that only makes you *more* of a hero. You must've jumped knowing you wouldn't survive the fall."

"I couldn't think about it."

Jennifer stared at me for a moment like she was sizing me up. And then she leaned forward and spoke quietly. "Now let *me* tell *you* a secret."

I leaned closer.

"It doesn't surprise me that Donald has a secret cave. I believe he's a man of a *million* secrets, the biggest one being . . . *How* did he get *his* power?"

I blinked. "Huh?"

"Think about it. He's not a descendant. And he's not one of the Seven Keys. He came *before* the Keys, right? So he *shouldn't* have a power."

Whoa. She was right.

How *did* he get his power?

"It's something I've always wondered," she said.

"Do you know the answer?"

". . . Maybe," she said, looking away and smiling. "But if I did, I couldn't tell you."

"Come on!" I said loud enough for the waitress to look at us from the back.

"Need another slice?" she asked.

Jennifer waved. "Nope, we're done."

"Do you think it was a super serum?" I asked. "Like, in a capsule? Or a gadget or . . . *a magic lamp*?"

Jennifer made a *"for real?"* face. "Just forget I said anything, okay? I don't want you getting any crazy ideas."

"Like I'm actually gonna do anything about it! But, like, where would he keep something like that? If he's still got it, I mean . . ."

"I don't know," Jennifer said as she got up. "That's a pretty big secret to keep hidden away."

Jennifer paid the bill, and we went outside to her Vespa.

"*If* it exists, then it's probably locked up," Jennifer said. "Somewhere nobody could find it, or even have access to it."

I hopped onto the back of her scooter.

"It was prob'ly in his cave!"

"We're not talking about this." Jennifer groaned. "Now hang on. This puppy's got some kick."

The Vespa sputtered forward, and we drove out of Lost Nation all the way back to the hidden school in the mountains.

A school created by a man with a million secrets.

And one of those secrets . . . might be the key to giving me a real superpower.

CHAPTER SIXTEEN

4 p.m.

The next day.

Miss Sweeney told us to meet her after school to see some files she had found from the early days of Kepler Academy—the ones we hoped would have more information about Fifteen. But to be honest, I was already on to the next mystery.

The *real* mystery was the one about Kepler's power.

I told my buds all about the Magic Lamp (that's what we're calling it now—tell your friends). They didn't believe it existed, but I couldn't blame them.

Even *I* knew it sounded too good to be true.

. . . right?

We were on our way to Miss Sweeney's office when we ran into Millie. Arnold and two other kids were with her.

"Just who I was looking for," Millie said. "Membership for the Braver Ravers *doubled* once everyone heard about how you spanked Dexter last night with your psychokinetic power."

"Yes, I *totally* did," I said, "with my pyscho . . . tronic power . . . and stuff."

"Why were you looking for Ben?" Penny asked.

I smelled a hint of jealousy.

Or maybe it was coffee.

Was someone brewing coffee?

"Our new members wanted to meet him and get his autograph!" Arnold said.

Noah and Jordan smiled. At least I *think* Jordan smiled. His body perked up.

I signed some notebook covers, and Millie took a picture of me posed like a superhero.

"Sooo *we* gotta go," Penny said, pulling on my arm. "We got that *thing* we needed to do. Remember?"

"Right," Noah said. "The *thing*."

Millie and the Braver Ravers said good-bye, and our groups went our separate ways.

Gotta be honest here . . .

I *really* liked having a fan club.

"I'm sorry, but this is the best I could do," Miss Sweeney said as we all stared at the nearly empty box on her desk.

"Is this from Year One?" Penny asked, riffling through vintage photos.

"I'm afraid not. You know, it's the strangest thing, but I can't find *anything* from Year One. All the other years are there—just not the first."

"Just Year One is missing, huh?" Noah whispered to me. "How *convenient*. And *inconvenient*. It's *both*. It can be both, right?"

Penny thanked Sweeney for her help and headed for the door with Noah and Jordan.

But I wasn't ready to duck out just yet.

"Hey, can I ask you a question about Headmaster Kepler?" I said to Sweeney.

My friends turned around. They knew what I was gonna ask because they had that *"Don't even do it"* look in their eyes.

"Of course you can," Sweeney said.

"How did he get his power?" I asked.

The teacher thought for a moment. "Well, from what I can remember, he did it through extensive testing and experimentation on himself."

"Okay, but what *kind* of experimentation?" I asked. "Like, he *gave* himself a power, right?"

"Subtle," Penny said quietly.

Sweeney furrowed her brow. "I believe you're correct, but I imagine the scientific details of his experiments are top secret. Otherwise, everyone in the world would give themselves a superpower—and we know how bad *that* would be."

I smiled.

That was enough for me.

Jennifer was onto something.

Sweeney confirmed it.

Kepler *gave* himself a power.

He wasn't born with one.

Just then, the school's intercom buzzed.

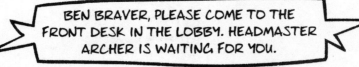

BEN BRAVER, PLEASE COME TO THE FRONT DESK IN THE LOBBY. HEADMASTER ARCHER IS WAITING FOR YOU.

GREAT...

CHAPTER SEVENTEEN

I was nervous.

I had no idea what was going on.

Headmaster Archer didn't say a word when I met him in the lobby. He just led me into the elevator and pushed the button for the tenth floor.

The doors scraped open, revealing a giant apartment. It was so big that it might've been the only thing on the tenth floor.

Headmaster Kepler stood at the far end of the room, goggling out the window, still wearing that strange contraption of lights on his head.

This was probably *his* apartment.

Comic book villains always live on the top floor.

It's how they roll.

But he wasn't alone.

Coach Lindsay sat on the couch, and the ghost of Professor Duncan floated in front of the fireplace.

I realized it was the first time I'd seen Duncan all year.

In case you missed my origin story—Professor Duncan was graced with the power of "not dying."

His *body* could die, and *did* die, but his soul refused to pass into the next life.

And last year he was a walking skeleton up until I *kinda sorta* shattered his bones.

That was my bad.

"Go on," Archer said, nudging me.

I walked through the room, making mental notes of everything I saw, but there really wasn't much. Except for some junky furniture, Kepler's apartment was pretty empty.

But then something strange caught my attention. Pinned to the fridge was a Polaroid photo of a short dude wearing an Elvis mask, standing in front of Campion's Diner. The current year was scribbled in marker at the bottom.

I was there, on my way to school, when that photo was taken.

What the heck was it doing in—

"Sit," Archer said, putting his hand on my shoulder. "Lindsay has some words to share about you."

Oh no. Coach must've had a change of heart.

I was getting busted for being in the city last night!

"I wasn't doing anything wrong!" I said. "I mean, I was just down there because—"

"*Sit!*" Coach said, not letting me finish.

I found a spot across from him.

Kepler mumbled something, then wobbled out of the room. I wasn't sure if he even knew we were there.

Archer folded his arms. "Your name was brought up during the staff meeting this morning."

"Am I in trouble?" I asked. "Don't I get a phone call? I want my phone call."

"No, you're not here because you're in trouble," Archer said. "You're here because Lindsay has suggested it might be good for you to work with Professor Duncan in his lab."

*Side note—not having a physical brain means Duncan's a supergenius, too. He spends most of his time inventing gadgets so redic that even *Batman* would be jealous.

"What, back on the roof?" I asked, super excited.

Archer shook his head. "No, that run-down shack is gone. You'll be working in his *actual* lab. *Under* the school."

I looked at the ghost, but he didn't say anything.

Why wasn't he saying anything?

"Are you okay with this?" I asked Duncan.

The ghost shrugged.

"Professor Duncan's had a long summer," Lindsay said. "He hasn't been himself lately."

"Because I'm *not* myself," Duncan drawled. "I'm just a shadow of a man. I can't interact with anything in this world. I can't turn on a TV . . . flip pages of a book . . . work in my lab."

Duncan was depressed.

The ghost continued. "I'm cursed as an eternal by-stander. When you die, I'll still be here. When the world ends, I'll still be here. And billions of years from now, when our sun fizzles out, I'll still be here. Alone and floating through space."

NAH, IT'LL PUT HAIR ON YOUR CHEST!

"Duncan's lost his will to live," Archer said, "which is ironic considering his circumstances. At any rate, he needs to feel like himself again, and that's where you come in. You have experience with his tools. You were very involved with his Wearable Tech club last year. You'd be perfect!" He leaned closer and whispered loudly, "Plus, you *kind of* owe it to him since it's *your* fault that he's like this."

Duncan finally looked at me. He had the face of a defeated child, sad and alone.

But there was a tiny bit of hope in his eyes.

He was waiting for my answer.

They all were.

Coach even winked at me.

He set this up. He must have, but why was he being so cool? It must've been something Jennifer said. Maybe she told him I didn't have a power, and this was his way of feeling sorry for me.

Whatever.

The *why* didn't matter.

I'd just been offered a chance to work in Duncan's lab under the school! That was like getting invited to the Batcave!

And who could say no to that?

MILLIE KEEGAN

SUPERPOWER: DREAM MANIPULATION
POWER LEVEL: ☆
WEAKNESS: BEING AWAKE

MILLIE INVADED MY DREAM WITH A SPACE SWAT TEAM, BUT IT WAS LIKE ONLY IN MY DREAM. I THINK HER POWER IS LIMITED TO ONLY MANIPULATING REALITY IN THE DREAM WORLD... I THINK.

ARNOLD SOLIS

SUPERPOWER: POWER THIEF
POWER LEVEL: ☆ ☆ ☆
WEAKNESS: UNSURE

ARNOLD CAN ABSORB OTHER PEOPLE'S POWERS BY BITING THEM LIKE HE'S SOME KIND OF POWER VAMPIRE. HE'S LIMITED TO BEING WITHIN BITING DISTANCE OF SUPERPOWERED KIDS, BUT RIDICULOUSLY HARMLESS WHEN HE'S NOT.

IF ARNOLD LEARNS HOW TO STEAL POWERS WITHOUT BITING, HE COULD BECOME THE MOST POWERFUL KID ON THE PLANET.

JOEL TRYNISKI

SUPERPOWER: PORTALS
POWER LEVEL: ☆ ☆
WEAKNESS: POOR EYESIGHT, AND EASILY TAKEN ADVANTAGE OF BECAUSE OF HIS NEED TO FIT IN

JOEL CAN OPEN PORTALS BETWEEN TWO PLACES VERY FAR APART. LAST YEAR HE COULD ONLY OPEN TEENY TINY PORTALS.

SOMETIMES HE SMELLS LIKE STALE BREAD.

CHAPTER EIGHTEEN

Mid-October.

Because of the Power Battles, I had started sketching stat cards for every kid in the school, giving star ratings and taking notes on weaknesses like we were in a giant Pokémon game.

The school probably kept those kinds of records, but it couldn't get into the dirty like I could.

I was with Brock, filling him in on pretty much everything.

". . . And then Jennifer said she was cool with the battles as long as they were low-key," I said to Brock. "You'd like her. She's really nice."

Brock was quiet, but he was never much of a talker.

"Everybody's got costumes and superhero names and everything!" I said. "It's crazy, but school this year is what I wish last year was like. I mean, the battles are mega–top secret from teachers, but that just makes it more real—like, secret lives and identities matter."

I sketched out another card.

"I'm also helping Duncan now, which is amazeballs. He hasn't told me when, but soon. I bet I'll get to test all kinds of cool stuff! Maybe I can even be the first kid in outer space!"

I took a second to soak it all in.

Life was looking so good I couldn't believe I was ever afraid of coming back.

CHAPTER NINETEEN

Late October.

Still no word from Duncan about working in his lab. I was starting to wonder if maybe *he* was waiting for *me* to say something.

In the meantime, the next Power Battle was starting in exactly thirty minutes.

Joel left a portal stretched open over the toilet seat in the third stall of the boys' locker room. He thought it'd be hilarious if everybody jumped *into* the toilet.

We walked out to the alley from the Kepler garage but were stopped before going into the factory next door.

"Ben!" a woman called. "Over here!"

It was Jennifer, chilling on her Vespa in the shadows.

"Jennifer!" I said, giving her a hug.

I'm not sure why I did that.

She wasn't sure, either.

"Oh, okay, hey there, kiddo," she said, awkwardly patting my back. "Nice to see you, too."

Penny folded her arms. "You must be *Jennifer*."

Jennifer grinned. "My reputation precedes me."

"Ben's told us *all* about how you rescued him in the alley. Pretty convenient how you were just *there*. Like, secret villain convenient."

"Hey," I said. "Jennifer saved my life!"

"No, Penny's figured me out," Jennifer said all sassy. "*I'm* the villain who was working with Abigail last year, but now that she's locked up, I've got nothing else to do but eat microwaved dinners and ride my scooter around Lost Nation 24/7."

The sarcasm was thick.

Jennifer continued. "If I were the villain, don't you think I'd be doing more villainy things than babysitting a bunch of kids?"

Noah shrugged at Penny.

Penny scowled. "Touché."

"What're you doing out here?" I asked.

"Making sure everyone's safe," she said. "I drive by

114

every night because I knew it was a matter of time before y'all came back."

Jennifer joined us as we went into the factory, where a bonkers Power Battle was already taking place. This time, there was a wrestling ring with ropes, except the ropes weren't *actual* ropes—they were toes. Toby's toes to be exact—stretchy toes was his power. His stank-nasty power.

The crowd was bigger than the first night, with more than a dozen costumed kids cheering from all sides like they were at a WWE match.

We hung back so Noah and Penny could get into costume.

Noah was a wizard.

Penny wore mouse ears that pushed her hair forward, framing her face, which brought more attention to her eyes.

It was *supes* cute.

But I didn't say that.

I didn't have a costume.

No need if I wasn't battling, right?

"These are good for students," Jennifer said, her eyes on the match. "There's no better way to sharpen powers than to actually use them. Kepler Academy doesn't understand that, which has led to many *preventable* accidents."

"Like Brock," I said.

Jennifer exhaled slowly. "Exactly like Brock. And his sister."

"Uh . . . Angel died in a car wreck," Penny said. "Her car exploded after she drove it off a bridge. Coach told us so."

"That's not entirely true," Jennifer said. "It was Angel that exploded—not the car. She freaked out, her power surged, and kaboom."

"Why would Coach lie about that?" I asked.

Jennifer chewed her lip for a moment. "Lindsay just wants to protect students. Kids would freak out if they knew about every single power-related death that's ever happened."

Millie's voice carried over the crowd as she ran from the ring to meet us. "Ben!"

Noah's jaw dropped as Millie arrived.

"Oh. My. Wow," Penny said.

"Can I get one of those?" Noah asked.

Millie beamed. "OMG, for sure! I'll make you one! You want one, too, Penny?"

"Absolutely, yes, of course I do," Penny said.

I couldn't tell if she was being snarky or not.

Millie turned to me, holding her hands together, fingers interlocked like she was begging. "Are you battling tonight?"

I froze up. "Uh, no, I went last time," I said all coolsies. "Other kids should have a turn."

"You're so humble. The most powerful kid in school

should be humble. And handsome, too. *Humble and handsome.*"

Penny choked on a laugh.

"The Braver Ravers had hoped you'd battle tonight, but it's cool," Millie said. "Next time, though, okay?"

"Totally!" I bragged. "I'm gonna *kill it* at the next battle—just wait and see. Hashtag, Braverboy. It's trending. Tell everyone!"

Whyyyy did I say that?

Millie pumped her fist. "*Heck, yes!* They're gonna be so excited!"

She skipped back to the ring.

Jennifer looked at me with wide eyes and an even wider smile. "So! The Braver Ravers?"

"Yeah." Penny smiled. "He's their hero. No bigs."

Jennifer studied the crowd. "I think it's more than that. They look up to you, Ben. When you jumped off the roof last year, you changed things. These kids aren't just at a Power Battle. . . . These kids mean business."

The battle in the ring ended, and the winner raised her hands, howling victoriously as the crowd went nuts.

"These kids aren't going down without a fight," Jennifer said proudly. She sniffed deeply, taking it all in. "It's amazing how similar this is to when I was in school—I mean, you guys are more hard-core, more *driven*. Our Power Battles were in the woods every Saturday at midnight, but they were *still* pretty intense. I don't want to toot my own horn, but my best friend and I dominated most of them."

I wished I could see what Jennifer was remembering, because her eyes were lit up as she stared into space.

Vic walked out to the center of the ring and announced the next battle. "Five minutes, people! Noah Nichols and Dexter Dunn, please report to the circle! The Wizard versus the Chill Pill! Five minutes, people!"

Noah punched his fists together. "Finally."

"Remember this *isn't* a fight. It's a *battle* between *powers*," Jennifer said. "Go easy on him."

"No way," Penny said. "Go crazy, God-mode-activated on him! Beat him so bad that his DNA passes the nightmares on to his children and his children's children! Make him *regret* coming tonight!"

Noah exhaled. "I just wanna have fun."

"Well, that, too," Jennifer said. "Whatever you do, just play it up for the crowd and give us a show!"

CHAPTER TWENTY

It was about to go down.

Noah and Dexter were in the ring, waiting for the battle to start as kids bet on who was going to win.

Jennifer watched from the entrance to make sure nobody came in.

DO SOMETHING NEW. SOMETHING WE HAVEN'T SEEN BEFORE!

BUT I DON'T KNOW ANYTHING NEW!

"You didn't learn *one new trick* over the summer?" Penny asked.

"Yeah, right! My parents would've *killed* me if I did that! They're pretty against my doing *anything* with my power."

Vic shouted from the side of the ring. "Battlers at the ready! Three—two—one . . ."

Dexter rolled his shoulders and craned his neck. His skin turned from pink to blue to crystal clear as he transformed into a solid-ice monster.

Apparently, *Dexter* was the one who learned a new trick over the summer.

"*Battle!*" Vic bellowed.

The ice monster stomped across the ring, shaking the whole factory with each step. He swung a slow, but powerful fist, which smashed against Noah's whole body, sending him bouncing off Toby's toe ropes.

"You even gonna try?" Dexter asked as he loomed over my friend. He put his hands together and then hammered down, serving a crushing blow to Noah.

That's when we heard a burp so loud the windows rattled. Fire bloomed around Dexter, turning into black smoke that mushroomed in the air above the ring.

The crowd gasped.

Dexter staggered back as gallons of water splashed across the concrete floor.

Noah had melted Dexter's arms off!

"Dude, are you okay?" Noah said, frantic. "OMG, OMG, OMG. I'm so sorry!"

Dexter grimaced, armless and angry. He lurched forward, growing two new icicle arms out of thin air, like no big deal. And then he threw a haymaker to end all haymakers.

Noah fired up his feet and tried to fly away, but Dexter grabbed his leg and pulled him back down.

Noah panicked. The fire from his feet became white-hot jet streams, rocketing the two boys straight up in the factory, breaking through the rusted, thin ceiling, and taking the battle out into the open sky.

Everyone ran outside to watch.

"What's Noah doing?" Jennifer said. "Is he crazy?"

"He's just trying to defend himself!" I said.

Noah and Dexter were still in midair. Two trails of fire followed Noah as he tried to shake Dexter off.

"You need to stop the battle!" Penny said to Jennifer, but Jennifer was already driving away on her scooter.

"Where's she going?" I said.

"Seriously?" Penny said. "She just left us?"

"He's falling!" someone shouted, pointing.

Noah had finally shaken the ice monster loose.

Vic held her arms out to try to stop Dexter's fall, but I think he was moving too fast. All she was able to do was slow him up a little bit until he crashed into the middle of the street . . . right in front of an oncoming car.

The driver swerved and skidded to a stop.

Nobody moved.

Dexter stood, unfazed by the fall. Then he saw the stopped car. "Uh-oh."

The doors opened, and some college kids stepped out, wearing Lost Nation University sweatshirts.

Dexter powered down, transforming back into his normal self as Noah eased into a soft landing next to him.

The college students had seen all of it.

Penny pulled on my shirt. "We gotta get outta here! *We gotta go!*"

"What about those guys in the car?" Millie asked.

"It's too late! We just need to leave!" Penny loudly commanded.

Everyone raced into the Kepler garage, to Joel's portal that opened into the boys' locker room back at the academy.

As soon as the last of us was through the portal, Joel slammed the toilet seat shut.

The locker room was dead silent.

Everyone stared at one another with a shared look of

"holy-crud-we-just-screwed-up-in-the-worst-epically-
disastrous-way-possible."

We had just gotten *caught*.

There were *witnesses*.

There were *people* who saw—

That's when Millie started laughing.

Other kids smiled until they couldn't take it anymore and burst out laughing, too.

Soon, the rest of us joined in.

Even Dexter and Vic wiped tears from their eyes.

Power Battles were unpredictable.

Unsafe.

Uncontrollable.

But they were a heck of a lot of fun.

CHAPTER TWENTY-ONE

Everything was cool the next day.

There was nothing on the news or the Internet about LNU students seeing superpowered kids.

And Coach Lindsay never said anything, either, which meant Jennifer hadn't told him. Probably not because she was being cool, but because she didn't want to lose her job.

After Noah's glorious Power Battle, I couldn't wait for Duncan to come to me anymore.

I had to go to him. I needed gear!

So I found him and asked him as politely as I could.

His confidence in me wasn't strong.

That's how the three of us found ourselves hiking through the forest behind the school.

"This is a dumb idea," Penny said. "Noah's battle was *intense*. What kinda *gadget* could you even use in the ring?"

"I don't know," I said. "But Duncan's gotta have *something* shibby."

"I'm with Penny on this one," Noah said. "Faking a power last year was okay because you didn't do anything with it, but now you're talking about using it against other kids?"

"It'll be fine! And it's just until I give myself an *actual* superpower."

"Right, with Kepler's Magic Lamp." Penny groaned. "You're starting to sound like a villain."

"No, I'm not! I *want* great responsibility," I said, "but first I need great power."

Penny stopped and pointed up ahead. "Is that . . . an ice-cream truck?"

It *was* an ice-cream truck, totally out of place, and totally sitting next to a log cabin.

"This must be the place," I said, hands on my hips.

"Not it!" Penny and Noah both snapped.

They looked at me.

"Way to take one for the team," Penny said. "Now go knock on that door, Braver."

"I hate you guys," I said.

The rotting stairs were uninviting, but I went up anyway.

"You think this is where Totes lives?" I said, about to knock, but the door opened before I could.

A hulking beast stood over me, at least eight feet tall, with white fur and a blue face.

"*I wanna pet that!*" Penny whispered.

"*What do you want?*" the monster growled.

"Nothing!" I said, choking on my tongue. "I mean, can I speak to Totes, please, sir? Ma'am? Thank you. . . . *Don't eat me.*"

Totes's voice came from inside the cabin. "Is it for me? Do I got visitors? Move your hairy butt, Doug! I got visitors!"

The fuzzy creature lumbered aside.

"Come on in, guys! Welcome to the zoo," Totes said, inviting us into his home, which was actually home to several different creatures, all watching TV in the living room.

"What's with the ice-cream truck?" I asked.

"Oh, you saw!" Totes said. "Always been a dream of mine to own one."

"A goat selling ice cream," Penny said. "Too funny."

"Who said anything about selling it?"

"What is this place?" Noah asked.

"This is where descendants go if they've permanently transformed," Totes said.

"Why not just go home?" I asked.

"You think we can go home like this? Doug turned into a *yeti*! That's a *fictional* animal!"

"Is that Ben Braver?" The cabin rattled as a kangaroo with dumbbells hopped into the room. "It *is* Ben Braver!"

I think of kangaroos as cute and cuddly.

Not this one.

This kangaroo was *jacked*.

Just insane muscles everywhere.

"Totes brags about you all the time," he said. *"Coolest kid in the school, everybody loves him, blah blah blah . . ."*

Totes stuck out his tongue. *"Meh!"*

"I'm Kang," the kangaroo said as he caressed his swole biceps. "So you're the kid who jumped off the school. Don't look like much, do you?"

"He's enough for *me*," Penny said. "Us. I mean, he's enough for *us*. Right, Noah?"

Kang snorted. "You got guts, kid, takin' on a monster like that, but you survived because of dumb luck."

"I *survived* because I'm psychotic," I said.

"Psychokinetic," Penny corrected. "No, y'know what? You were right the first time."

"Fine," Kang said, flexing his pecs one at a time. "You stopped Abigail, but you can't stop the future."

"What's *that* supposed to mean?" I asked.

"Abigail's victory is changing the world. She's the little pebble creating all the ripples."

The kangaroo sounded like Kepler.

"Abigail didn't win," Penny said. "Ben beat her."

"Ben stopped her from destroying a building, but her goal was to send a message, and every descendant in the world heard it."

"What message?" Penny said.

"That we don't have to hide in cabins and cubicles anymore," Kang said, doing curls with the dumbbells.

His weight lifting was making me all sorts of uncomfortable.

"A couple of descendants even played superhero over the summer," Totes said. "Capes and powers and everything."

"No," Penny said. "That'd be all over the news."

"The school works overtime to keep a lid on it. Won't be long, though," Kang said as he kissed his deltoid. "Do you know how famous I'm gonna get? Have you *seen* my abs?"

The kangaroo blew out air as his midsection tightened.

I mean, honestly, he had great abs.

Totes shook his head. "What do you guys need?"

"Uh, so Duncan's letting us in his lab," I said. "He told me you'd know what that means."

"Gotcha. BRB."

Totes left the room, leaving us alone with the beefcake kangaroo who wouldn't shut up.

"You wanna know the *real* threat?" he asked. "The Abandoned Children."

"Who are the Abandoned Children?" I asked.

Noah and Penny looked uneasy.

They knew the answer.

"Ex-Kepler students who've gone off the radar," Kang said.

Totes returned with a skull hanging from his horn.

"They're a buncha crazies who believe the world ended in the sixties."

"But the world *didn't* end," I said.

"Tell *them* that," Totes said, leading us out the door. As we headed back to the academy, Totes joked with Penny and Noah.

I didn't say much.

The world was going to change—Jennifer said it first, and now the beefcake kangaroo said the same thing.

Hopefully, it wouldn't be for the worse.

CHAPTER TWENTY-TWO

Thirty minutes later.

Totes led the way with a flashlight in his mouth and a skull on his head.

We were somewhere *beneath* the basement of the school, walking down a concrete hallway nobody knew existed, accessed through a secret entrance disguised as a broken water fountain.

The top-secret-government-bunker décor gave me chills, and I realized I still had some fear of worm-eaters left inside me. I couldn't shake the feeling that they were going to jump out at me any second.

We finally made it to the entrance to the lab, where the concrete walls molded against a black metal door lined with tubes.

"*Duncaaan!*" Totes shouted.

The ghost floated through the door. "No need to shout, I'm right—" Duncan stopped. *"Quit wearing my skull like a hat!"*

Totes dropped the skull into my hands, then trotted away, but not without mumbling, *"Quit wearing my skull . . . I'm just a dead guy with no body . . . I'm smarter than everyone . . . blehhh . . ."*

Duncan told me to point his skull toward the door.

A red laser beam scanned the skull up and down.

Air pushed through invisible seams. The door slid up and out of view like something from *Star Wars*.

"My biometric data grant me entry," Duncan said. "I'll scan all yours, too, so you each can have access."

As soon as I walked inside, I *literally* died.

But not the *for-real* literally.

The *other* kind of literally.

I didn't actually die.

Gadgets and gizmos sat on a round table in the middle of the room, labeled and everything! Shelves along the walls were loaded to the edge with cool technological toys.

I didn't think I could get any happier.

I was wrong.

The walls came alive with holographic displays that would make Mission Control at NASA jealous. Colorful images danced around the lab, begging to be touched.

I brought my hand up, and—

"Don't," Duncan said. "Touch the wrong thing and you might explode."

We all looked at the ghost.

"No, seriously," Duncan said. "You wanna be known as the incredible exploding kid? Go ahead and touch away, friend."

I stuffed my hands into my pockets. "Fine."

"You three should consider yourselves lucky,"

Duncan said. "The only people ever allowed in here are Donald and me."

"*Nobody* else?" I said. "Why not?"

Duncan took a slow breath. "There are things in here that the world isn't ready for. Powerful things. *Dangerous* things. Things *real* bad guys would love to play with. Only a handful of people are trusted with the knowledge that this room even exists, and even *they* can't be allowed in."

"But you just let three random kids in," Penny said with a raised eyebrow. "Your security sucks."

"Quite honestly—I think I need this more than you," Duncan said. "I haven't . . . I haven't been doing so well lately, and getting back to old habits might help."

If I could've given that ghost a hug, I would've.

Duncan continued. "Ben, I have a lot of unfinished projects that you can be my hands for. I'll look over your shoulder while telling you how to work on them."

"A helicopter parent." Penny groaned.

"Helicopter parenting is cool with me as long as I get to play with Duncan's toys," I said.

Duncan chuckled slightly.

It was nice to see him smile.

I ran my fingers along the walls of the lab, which were made of black metal that looked wet but wasn't. "Are the walls Trutanium?" I asked.

"*Very* perceptive, Ben," Duncan said. "Ninety-nine

percent of all Trutanium is right here in this room, y'know."

"Where's the other one percent?"

"Keeping the world safe," Duncan said. "Would you mind opening this one for me?"

Several cardboard boxes sat under the table, but Duncan was pointing at only one. I slid the box out and tore into it like it was my birthday.

My jaw dropped.

I was speechless, which *rarely* happens.

"You like?" Duncan asked. "They're prototype super-suits. Each suit has a different function. The one on top is an antigravity suit. It's kind of my baby."

I reached inside and carefully removed Duncan's child from its cardboard womb.

It was just my size.

Pretty sure a tear fell from my face.

I THINK I HEAR ANGELS...

"Antigravity? Does it make you fly?" I said.

"No, no, no, it *shoots* antigravity pulses. It makes objects defy gravity," Duncan said.

"Why's it so small?" I said.

Duncan gave me a look. "It's not *small*. It's *my* size. I built it for myself when I was still a skeleton."

"And how old were you when you became a skeleton?" Noah asked.

". . . Twelve."

I wanted to scream, *"No way, I'm twelve right now!"* but that would've been ridiculously obvious.

So instead, I just whispered, "It's perfect . . ."

"Perfect for what?" Duncan asked, suspicious. *"Don't get any ideas, mister."*

The professor had every right to be suspicious . . . because I was getting *all* the ideas.

CHAPTER TWENTY-THREE

"**G**ame point, sucka," Jordan said, bouncing a Ping-Pong ball on his paddle. "I win this, I get your bed."

"No, you don't!" I said. "Stop making bets at game point!"

We were in the Kepler Academy game room, which was filled with students killing time on a monumentally boring Saturday afternoon.

Noah and Penny ate popcorn as they watched from the side.

Jordan served, and I swooped my paddle, slapping the ball just right to give it a wicked spin—a move my dad taught me.

Too bad I swung too hard.

The paddle slipped out of my hand and torpedoed into the back of some girl's head across the room.

"*Ouuuuuch!*" she howled.

It was Darla Dunn—a tenth grader who also happened to be Dexter's sister.

Darla and I had first met in Kung Fu Club last year,

when she used me to show everyone how much damage a fist can do to someone's face.

The answer is *a lot*, in case you're wondering.

Darla glared at me since Jordan was straight-up pointing at the kid who did it.

Not good.

Darla marched right up to me.

Jordan ducked under the table.

Noah and Penny continued eating popcorn.

"You did that on purpose!" Darla said, suddenly morphing into a giant centaur out of nowhere.

. . .

You read that right.

Darla turned into a half-horse woman.

It dawned on me that I didn't know what power Darla had.

She reached for me, but I shimmied across the table and rolled off the other side.

"It was an accident!" I said, turning to face the centaur, but to my surprise, it was gone.

Instead, an angry leprechaun was running straight at me, green sparkly suit and everything.

"*You're dead meat!*" the leprechaun wailed in Darla's voice.

The leprechaun was Darla!

Darla was a shape-shifter!

She jumped off the table and tackled me.

Noah and Penny just watched, and I couldn't blame them. I was in the middle of a beatdown, and even *I* was bewitched by her power!

Kids applauded as Darla transformed into a fat, hairy, heaving gorilla. She pulled me in and hugged me tighter and tighter until I couldn't breathe, and suddenly it wasn't so cool anymore.

"Let him go!" Penny said.

Jordan ran out of the room.

Noah jumped up, hungry for action, but before he did anything, a giant tentacle slammed down on the Ping-Pong table, breaking it in half.

Darla stopped. ". . . Wut?"

Everyone else stopped, too, staring at the girl with tentacles under her arms. She was wearing one of the "HERO" shirts with my face on it.

Behind her were Arnold, Millie, and the rest of the Braver Ravers.

"Put him down!" Millie commanded.

Darla dropped me. "You want some, too?"

The room was silent.

It was the calm before the storm.

And all of it was for me. How cool is that?

All at once, the Braver Ravers rushed past Millie, firing off their powers at Darla.

Arnold and Noah helped me to my feet.

"Stay back," Arnold said to me. "If you use your power, you'll get in trouble!"

Arnold took off and ran at Dexter's sister.

Everyone cheered like it was a Power Battle.

Darla caught Arnold with her gargantuan gorilla hands. He twisted and turned, then finally bit down on her hairy arm.

She instantly morphed back into a human as Arnold absorbed her power. And then Arnold transformed into an oversize tiger, roaring so loudly that I might've peed a little.

Just then, a furious Coach Lindsay burst through the door with Jordan by his side.

"That's enough!" Coach commanded.

Everyone muzzled up. Arnold turned back into a human.

Coach Lindsay rounded up Darla and most of the Braver Ravers—the ones who used their powers—and took them to detention for the rest of the day.

It took a second for it to hit me, but they were getting punished because of a stupid mistake that *I* made.

"Why'd they do that?" I said to Millie. "They got into trouble helping me."

"Yeah," Millie said. "They knew they would."

"Well, that was dumb," Penny said.

Millie glared at Penny. "Don't you get it yet? Ben isn't just a hero. He's a living legend. We're lucky to even be alive at the same time as him."

Noah smiled. "Yeah, Pen. We're lucky to even be in Ben's presence."

"Aww," Penny joined in on the joke, giving me puppy dog eyes.

"The Braver Ravers aren't just a fan club," Millie said. "We're a team, and Ben is our leader, and we'll protect him no matter what."

"Like junior X-Men!" I said. "Love it!"

"Or like a *gang*," Jordan said. "Do you love *that*?"

Millie laughed, like, *"You're crazy!"*

So did I.

I had to admit, having my own superhero squad sounded pretty dope.

All I'd have to do was *not* screw it up.

And how hard was that?

CHAPTER TWENTY-FOUR

Late November.

I t was colder than penguin poop outside, but that didn't
stop me from visiting Brock.

It was a good place to be alone, which also meant I
could work on stat cards in peace.

"There were all kinds of supersuits in there," I
said, "and one that looked like it was plucked right out

of an Avengers movie! And the best part? *It's a boy's huskyyyyy*—just my size!"

Brock was stone-cold quiet.

"I haven't tried it on yet," I said, "but I will before the next Power Battle on Christmas Eve."

The wind picked up a bit.

I thought about Jennifer.

The last time I saw her, she was driving away on her scooter.

"I hope she's not mad at us," I said, blowing hot air into my hands. "I wish I had a way to contact her, then I could tell her I finally got into Duncan's lab and—"

I jumped to my feet.

"Holy donks, the Magic Lamp! If it's real, then it's probably in there, right? I mean, who's it gonna hurt if I just *look* for it? It's not like I'm gonna *take* it or anything."

Brock silently agreed, and then he silently encouraged me to go find it.

And who was I to argue with a dead kid?

CHAPTER TWENTY-FIVE

The laser scanned my face, and the lab door slid open.

"Hello?" I said.

No answer was the best answer.

The door shut as I tiptoed like some kind of cat burglar to the table with all the gizmos. The whole thing *sorta* made me feel like I was the bad guy, but my intentions were good. So those things canceled each other out.

It's all about finding balance.

Unused holopods leaned against the wall—the same as the ones that hid the school outside.

Like a kid in a toy store, I switched one on. It flickered to life and then showed my mirror image standing at my side.

When I pointed the holopod at the table, half of it disappeared. I stepped through the invisible wall. Everything was still there—just hidden.

I drooled over the buffet of gadgets. What would the Magic Lamp even look like? I'd been calling it the Magic

Lamp so long that I imagined an actual genie-in-a-bottle oil lamp.

I started sliding boxes out from under the table. Each one was filled with junk I didn't recognize. Tools I've never seen before, etched with writing that looked . . . alien.

And none of it was labeled.

It was weird enough to give me the creeps.

The last box finally had labels.

They were all fancy and official-looking.

Project Blackwood was heavy and made of Trutanium.

Brock's last name was Blackwood—I wondered if it had anything to do with him. Was Duncan trying to bring him back to life? But it wasn't the Magic Lamp, so I tossed it back and shut the box.

Just then, the lab door opened.

I spun around as Donald Kepler faltered in, wearing his jammies and redonkulous hat. "... *Mustn't cause ripples ... mustn't stir the pot ...*" he murmured, never making eye contact.

He didn't know I was there.

The holopod was hiding me!

Duncan floated through the wall. He pointed to a bundle of cables hanging from the ceiling. "You need to take the green one and plug it into your helmet."

Kepler took the green cable and stuck it to the side of his helmet, twisting until the bulbs on top glowed brighter. His eyes rolled back as he swayed slightly.

Duncan glanced at the holopod.

It was out of place, and he knew it.

"Who's there?" he asked, staring past me.

Busted.

"Sorry," I said, stepping through the invisible wall with my head down.

Kepler flinched, gasping like he had just gotten caught.

"Relax," Duncan said. "It's only Ben."

"...*Who?*" Kepler barked.

"*Ben! Ben Braver!*" Duncan said, almost shouting.

"...*What if it's not JUST Ben Braver?*" Kepler slurred as he carefully approached me.

The old man grabbed the sides of my head, smooshed his nose against my noggin, and sniffed long and deep.

Kepler exhaled. "...*You're not him....He hasn't escaped....*"

What the heck was he on about?

"Who hasn't escaped?" I asked.

"...*The Reaper...*"

The Reaper?

The villain in the fake articles from the Kepler Cave?

Duncan cleared his throat loudly. "Ben, why are you here alone? The buddy system needs a buddy, or it's not a buddy system. What would happen if you got hurt and your buddy wasn't around? Huh, buddy?"

"Okay, I get it," I said. "Just stop saying *buddy*."

"But seriously," Duncan said. "I don't like this. The buddy system is for safety, but it's also for accountability. I know you'd never steal anything from me, but . . . I mean, Benzilla happened last year because you *took* one of my discs."

"Not on purpose!" I said. "I just . . . forgot it was in my pocket. It was an accident."

Duncan nodded. "Right, that's fine. I just don't want another *accident*."

Kepler's helmet dinged, and he yanked the cable out, trying not to lose his balance.

"Donald, we need to get you back to your room, okay?" Duncan said.

The old man nodded as he straggled back to the door.

Duncan followed but stopped to look back at me. "Put the holopod away," he said. "Get back to your room, and don't come back down here without a buddy."

I sighed as I turned off the holopod.

Not sure what was going on with Kepler, but pretty sure it made me sad. I didn't like seeing him like that.

I slid the cardboard boxes back under the table and scanned the room one last time. That was it—I had looked at every single thing in Duncan's lab.

If the Magic Lamp existed, it wasn't in there.

Bummer.

CHAPTER TWENTY-SIX

Christmas Eve.

Fifteen minutes until the next Power Battle, and I was ready to rock. Duncan's antigravity supersuit, which had less fabric than I originally thought, fit snug as a bug under my clothes.

I still wasn't sure exactly how to work the suit, but I was sure it would be easy.

Millie told Joel to open his portal earlier than usual that night so the Braver Ravers could go down and set things up.

I wondered if Jennifer would be there. I wasn't sure since it was Christmas Eve, and she was probably with family.

I was wrong.

She was waiting for us in the alley.

"How'd you know we'd be here?" I asked.

"I told you," Jennifer said, "I drive by every night. I saw kids, and I parked."

"Sorry about last time," I said.

"Why?" Jennifer said. "It wasn't *your* fault."

"Right," Noah said. "It was mine."

"It wasn't *anybody's* fault—the battle just got a little out of control. It happens."

"Why'd you just leave us like that?" I said.

Jennifer laughed. "Would you believe I just panicked and ran?"

I smiled. "We all did the same thing."

Penny looked around the dark alley as snow started falling. "Why aren't you home with your family? It's Christmas."

"If I *had* family, then I'd be home with them," Jennifer said. "But . . . my family's gone now."

"Ohhh," Penny said awkwardly.

"Hello?" someone said from the end of the alley—a teenager with a few of his buddies behind him. "Is this where KA-POW is?"

None of us knew what he was talking about.

"What's KA-POW?" Jennifer asked.

"Like, an underground wrestling thing or something," he said.

Jennifer's face turned red. "It's Christmas Eve. Everything's closed. Go home, dude."

"But we got a Facebook invite that said it was—"

Hoots and hollers came from inside the factory.

The Power Battle had started.

"Oh, cool, it *is* here," the teen said.

He and his buddies walked into the building full of top secret superpowered kids.

Jennifer shook her head, groaning. "I better get in there to make sure this hasn't gotten out of hand."

The three of us followed behind her, shocked at what we saw.

The crowd that night was the biggest by far, and not all of them were Kepler students.

The teens we followed were waiting at a table, where Millie was taking admission.

"Text your friends!" she said, counting bills. "Share my Facebook invite and get a dollar off!"

I could hear Jennifer's teeth grinding. *"She put the name of the academy right in the title."*

When Millie saw me, she stood on her chair and belted, "Ladies and gentlemen! I present to you—*Braverboooy!*"

Everybody cheered.

And by everybody, I mean only the Braver Ravers.

Millie ran over with a gift-wrapped box. "I made you something for your match tonight!" She gave me the cheesiest smile ever, pecked my cheek, and then ran back to the admission table.

All I could do was confusingly shrug as Penny stared daggers at me.

Inside the box was a cape that smelled like Millie had sprayed it with perfume. Wrapped in the cape was a custom plush doll of Braverboy.

"Holy goats!" Noah said. "Millie brought Totes!"

I turned and couldn't even.

Like, I *literally* could not even.

Totes, the goat who hated giving people rides, was in his own little booth . . . *giving people rides* for two bucks a pop.

"This is a circus," Jennifer said.

The crowd *"ohhh'd!"* at the two kids in the Power Battle. Noah and Penny rushed to catch the end of the match. I tried, but Jennifer pulled me back, and she did *not* look happy.

"Ben, this needed to be low-key," she said. "I can

ignore a few kids in an empty building, but you got a whole audience here! *There's a goat giving rides!*"

Why was she getting mad at *me*?

"I didn't do this!" I said. "Millie's the one who—"

"Don't! The old man *hates* attention, which means *I* hate attention, and this? *This* is *attention! This* is on the edge of getting outta hand. I can't keep this a secret if *half* the city knows about it!"

"*But—*"

"If *I* don't report this to Lindsay, *I'll* be in just as much trouble as you!" Jennifer said. "You're putting me in a *terrible* position, Ben!"

"*I'm not—*" I said, wanting to defend myself, but I couldn't.

Vic shouted from the ring. "Five minutes, people! Ben Braver and Christie Tigerlilly, please report to the ring! Braverdork versus the Snot Rocket! Five minutes, people!"

I was next up in the Power Battle.

CHAPTER TWENTY-SEVEN

Five minutes later, I stood in the ring, opposite of Christie Tigerlilly—a.k.a. the Snot Rocket, a sixth grader who I hadn't met yet.

THE SNOT ROCKET

Just like the first time I was in the ring, Millie started a chant, but this time they were saying, "*Brav-er-boy! Brav-er-boy! Brav-er-boy!*"

I think she wanted me to be a superhero even more than I did.

After stripping down to my supersuit, I stood at the

side of the ring, feeling a draft on my inner thighs since Duncan's suit was less of a full-body suit and more of a woman's bathing suit.

The Snot Rocket mean-mugged me, finger under her nose to keep snot from dripping.

We walked out to the center and bumped fists.

"Hi, I'm Ben."

"*I am the Snot Rocket!*" Christie shot back.

"Yeah, no, I'm *Braverboy*, but my real name's Ben. And you're Christie, right?"

She curled her lip. *"I am the Snot Rocket."*

Clearly she wasn't gonna break character.

Good for her.

I waved to the Braver Ravers. They jumped like baby

birdies, reaching for me like I was their mama about to puke some food into their tiny empty beaks.

Wait, no, that's—forget I said that.

"*Battle!*" Vic proclaimed.

The Snot Rocket sneered and pulled a thick rope of yellow snot out of her nose.

It was so gross it was probably illegal.

Everyone squirmed.

Pretty sure someone in the back barfed.

The Snot Rocket whipped her rope at me like she was Indiana Jones in the Temple of Doom. I somersaulted out of the way as her lung butter slapped the floor like fresh guacamole.

"My turn," I said, secretly activating my supersuit by slapping the gloves together.

I waited.

She waited.

The crowd waited.

I had no idea how to work the suit.

Christie jammed her thumb against a nostril and blew, firing off actual rockets of snot across the ring.

The first couple skimmed past me, but the rest of her

nose nuggets splashed against my neck, exploding in a soggy mess of nastiness.

I ran around the ring, clapping my hands over and over, trying to get the suit to activate, but it just looked like I was giving myself a round of applause.

My opponent came at me screaming like a banshee, carrying a softball-size snot bomb that she smashed into my face. Snot filled my eyes, my nose, my mouth . . . every hole in my head!

I fell to the ground, still trying to get Duncan's stupid suit to work.

Christie towered over me, snorting deeply, preparing her finishing move.

And then it happened.

The suit activated.

The fabric cinched up and tickled my skin with what felt like humming. I still wasn't sure exactly how to shoot an antigravity pulse, but Christie helped me figure it out real quick.

She craned her neck, tightened her lips, and blew her nose hard, sending a tidal wave of wet boogies my way.

I aimed my hands at her and pushed my fingers out, feeling energy zap out of my gloves. I shut my eyes and let loose a barrage of blasts, hoping *one* would hit her.

People screamed as chairs clanged.

Penny shouted, "*Stop!*"

Noah shouted, "*Keep going!*"

Totes shouted, "*No free rides!*"

I finally dropped my hands, and the blasts stopped.

I opened one eye.

Christie floated helplessly a few feet off the ground. So did the rest of the crowd behind her side of the ring.

I turned to face the kids behind me, who were still standing. Saucer-eyed and jaws dropped, they gazed at me in awe. The teens who had come in were blown away.

"Best battle ever!" Arnold declared.

Millie grabbed my arm and held it up. *"Braverboy for the win!"*

Everyone went ballistic, jumping up and down, chanting my superhero name.

Noah and Penny smiled from ear to ear.

Dexter was fuming.

I did it.

I was the winner.

I mean, that's what I planned on doing the whole time, but I couldn't believe I actually did it!

I was awesome. Amazing. Remarkable.

I was unstoppable!

I jumped as high as I could. *"HECK YEAH, I'M THE ULTIMATE CHAMPION OF THE UNIVERSE!"*

I was on top of the world.

And nothing could bring me down.

CHAPTER TWENTY-EIGHT

Mid-January.

"Ah, you should've seen it!" I said to Brock, still reeling about my completely colossal grand slam at the last Power Battle. "Kids were all over me for autographs."

I threw a couple of punches into the cold night air, making sure I was in full view of the North Star, because it felt like I was showing off for my dad.

"I'm, like, the coolest kid in school right now! Everybody wants a piece of me, *or* they want to *be* me! I can't believe I was such a *lamewad* at the beginning of this year. I wish I could go back in time and tell that scared little baby Ben how awesome he'd be by the end of the semester!"

Brock agreed, obviously.

"This is what I've always wanted, dude . . . if only my parents could see me now."

I found the North Star and stared at it.

"Can't wait to tell them when I get home. They're gonna be *so* proud of me. I mean, not for faking a superpower, but for getting over my fear."

I sat on the stone snake, catching my breath.

I was afraid for so long—afraid of failing, of worm-eaters, of what other kids thought of me—that I almost forgot what it was like to just be chill.

I liked this feeling.

It was a feeling I hadn't had in a long time.

I wasn't afraid anymore.

Nailed it.

CHAPTER TWENTY-NINE

Late January.

Time flies when you're having fun, and the amount of fun I was having was off the flippin' charts.

I was a king.

I didn't have to carry my own books anymore.

I didn't have to buy my own snacks anymore.

Pretty sure I wouldn't even have to wipe my own butt anymore, but that's just—that's too far. *Way* too far.

I could sit anywhere I wanted at lunch, and any place I picked would instantly swarm with students who loved me.

It was so much fun that January breezed by like a fart in the wind. Soon it was time for the next KA-POW.

I walked into the factory with my boys— Noah, Jordan, and new recruit Arnold— behind me.

Penny wasn't with us.

She was doing that a lot lately. I think she was just annoyed with the big crowds that worshipped me.

I mean, why else would she avoid me like that, right?

People were everywhere. Kepler students and random teens from the city eating snacks, waiting for the battle to begin under the giant KA-POW banner.

My face adorned the shirts of many that night.

More than I'd like to admit were I a humble man.

But I'm not humble.

And it was a *ton* of shirts.

I looked for Jennifer, but she wasn't there. Not sure if that was a good thing or not. Last time we talked, she scolded *me* for how big the Power Battle had grown, like it was *my fault* that happened. She'd totally change her tune if she could only see how much everyone loved me now—I think. I dunno—it made sense in my head.

The Braver Ravers waved me over to the ring. Millie had found a cruddy, old couch in one of the back rooms and set it up in the front row.

Someone handed me a pop as soon as I sat down, but it was flat, so I sent it back.

"Don't even bring me another one if it's not fresh!" I said.

Noah gave me a look.

"What?" I said.

"Nothing, man. It's just . . . That kid brought you a soda, and you yelled at him for it."

"Not enough suds, bro!"

Noah shook his head, and then he got off the couch.

"Where you going?" I said.

He shrugged his shoulders. "I just—I can't. You're too much."

"What's that supposed to mean?" I said, but Noah was already gone.

"It means you're being a thick jerk," Jordan said, right before he left the couch, too.

I laughed.

My friends were so funny.

Penny climbed through Toby's toe ropes with her costume and uke.

Millie went out to join her.

"Geez, nobody wants to wrestle that guy," Millie said. "I need to find someone else for you to battle then."

"I'll go!" Arnold said, shooting his arm up.

"Fine, get up here," Millie said, and then she yelled, "Um, five minutes until the first battle! Penny Plum versus Arnold Solis! The Creature Queen versus the Mooch! Five minutes!"

"Where's Vic?" Arnold asked. "She always announces."

"I don't know; I couldn't find her," Millie said. "Dexter's not here, either."

Penny plucked the strings on her uke, tuning it by ear.

"Go, Penny!" I said loudly. "You got this, guurl!"

Arnold looked over, like, *What about me?*

"Uh, you got this, too . . . *guuuy.*"

The kid with the flat pop returned with a second one, and the amount of fizz was pleasing to me this time.

Yes, I was pleased.

With the soda.

With my seat.

With my life.

Millie made the announcement.

And the battle began.

CHAPTER THIRTY

Penny danced along the sides of the ring, tickling the strings on her ukulele.

Arnold made some *"gonna getchoo"* thrusts but never went into full attack mode. With his ability to steal someone else's power, all he needed was patience.

The Braver Ravers around me cheered loudly for Arnold, but Noah and Jordan loyally supported Penny from the other side of the ring.

I didn't know who to root for.

If Penny, then the Braver Ravers would be mad.

If Arnold, then Noah and Jordan would be mad.

So I watched quietly.

Arnold dashed toward Penny, chomping his teeth, but she bounced off the rope, flipping right over him. When she landed, she threw her hair back and strummed wildly.

Someone screeched from the back of the room.

Then a whole line of people screeched, and the crowd quickly parted.

Penny must've called her army of mice.

I expected to see a hundred cute, button-nosed vermin charging the ring, but instead—

"*CHICKENS!*" somebody shouted.

Flocking to the ring was a platoon of poultry, clucking and flapping wildly. The birds gunned for Arnold, who was understandably frozen in place.

Penny climbed a corner of the ring, propped her foot up, and twirled her head as she ripped a killer solo on her small uke.

The chickens stacked on top of one another, forming a human-shaped walking chicken Voltron monster.

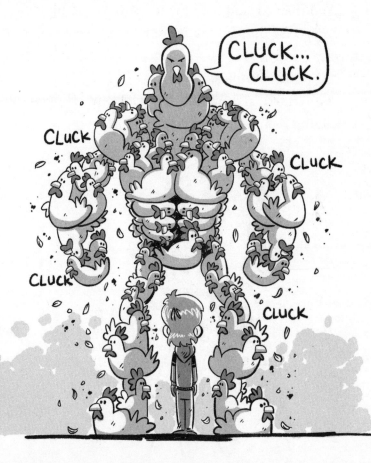

Penny soaked in the crowd's praise, having chicken-man take a bow. But her showmanship became her downfall.

Arnold broke through the wall of birds and tore across the ring straight for Penny. He grabbed her leg and gnawed on her calf.

Penny dropped her uke and fell off the ropes.

The chickens tumbled down, clucking and confused.

And then Arnold took the uke and began playing.

In precise unison, the fat birds snapped their beaks toward Penny.

"Ah, spit," Penny said.

As Arnold strummed, the chickens flipped out, swarming Penny as she screamed.

"*Hey!*" Noah shouted at Arnold. "Penny didn't make them peck at *you!*"

My best friend was in trouble.

Good thing I had my supersuit under my clothes.

I powered up and slid to the rescue under Toby's toes.

My fan club cheered for me, but other Kepler students weren't too happy that I crashed someone else's battle.

I shot an antigravity blast at the cluster of chickens that sent them flying, and then I held my hand out to my damsel in distress.

She wasn't as grateful as I thought she'd be.

"*What're you doing?*" Penny said.

"I'm rescuing you!"

"*I don't need to be rescued, Ben! Get outta the ring and let me handle this!*"

Students flooded the stage to pull me out.

The Braver Ravers ran in to stop them.

The one-on-one battle between Penny and Arnold quickly became a no-holds-barred Royal Rumble with superpowered kids.

Plus the chickens.

OMG, the chickens . . .

It was a chaotic mess of fire and ice. Lightning and thunder. Beaks and feathers.

It was out of control.

I crawled across the ring, trying to get to safety, but more kids piled on top of me.

Windows shattered when power blasts missed their targets. Factory machines collapsed. Concrete crumbled. The entire building shook, floors and walls and everything.

This was bad.

Worse than Noah and Dexter in the street.

And then someone grabbed my ankle.

It was Arnold, and he had a huge smile.

I tried to wiggle free, but his grip was too strong.

He pushed my pant leg up.

And then he bit me.

I shouted in pain as he laughed like it was all some kind of joke. But his laughter suddenly stopped. He stared at me, puzzled.

His power was absorbing other people's powers.

What happens if there's no power to absorb?

I saw the exact second he figured me out.

It was in his eyes.

Suddenly all the lights came on with a loud *CHUNK!*, and a large door at the front clanged open. Headmaster Archer and Coach Lindsay marched inside, shouting orders at students as they froze in place.

That's why Jennifer wasn't there—she was too busy snitching on the Power Battle.

But then I saw the *real* snitch stroll through the door with a smug smile. He tapped the headmaster's shoulder and pointed at the ring.

Headmaster Archer's eyes homed in on me, and his face grew bright red. If we were in a cartoon, steam would've been shooting out of his ears.

I was wrong.

It wasn't Jennifer who snitched.

It was Dexter.

CHAPTER THIRTY-ONE

Midnight.

Headmaster Archer's office.

I was in the headmaster's office, getting scolded by Headmaster Archer and Coach Lindsay.

I'd never seen Archer so mad, but honestly, he had only half my attention. The other half was worried about what Arnold was gonna do with my secret.

"Do you know how long it's going to take to wipe

the minds of all those people?" Archer said furiously. *"I don't like doing it!"*

"Because of all the vomit?" Duncan asked, floating through the door. "Mind-wiping ends with a lot of vomit."

"Do you know he's wearing one of your suits under his clothes right now?" Archer said.

Duncan turned slowly to face me. "Which one?"

"The antigravity one," I mumbled.

"Did you use it?"

"Yes . . ."

Duncan spoke calmly and quietly, which was only more upsetting. "Are you freaking kidding me right now? Do you know how lucky you are that you didn't rip anybody apart with that thing?"

"I didn't know it was that powerful," I said.

"Thankfully, Dexter Dunn had the right mind to tell me about the battle," Archer said. "Of *all* people! *Dexter! Dunn!"*

"Is this really a big deal?" Lindsay asked. "Power Battles are an unofficial tradition. Let's focus on the positives—student kidnappings are down *one hundred percent* compared with last year. Give Ben detention for using the suit and send him on his way."

Archer's death stare turned to Lindsay. "None of this would've happened if you'd done your job!"

"My job?" Lindsay repeated. "My *job* is to make sure this school isn't attacked by Abigail's partner!"

"Do we even know if Abigail was actually working with someone?" Duncan asked.

"No," Lindsay said. "We *don't*, but it's not my *job* to know that. All I need to do is keep the school and its students safe."

"Which can't happen if the students aren't even *at* the school!" Archer said loudly.

"*How can I possibly keep track of every single student?*" Coach said even louder.

I wondered how much Coach actually knew—if Jennifer told him anything about the Power Battles or if this was all new to him. It probably wasn't the best time to ask.

"I don't know why Donald even allowed you to attend this year," Archer said to me. "We're wiping your mind, and you're going home *tonight*. In fact, maybe we'll wipe you from the minds of everyone here. It'll be like you never even existed!"

My stomach sank. "You can't do that! Headmaster Kepler told me I could stay!"

"Ray, that's too harsh," Lindsay said. "The battle isn't *Ben's* fault. He didn't *organize* the event."

"Maybe not, but he's certainly the mascot!" Archer said, holding up a Braverboy doll.

"*That* wasn't me!" I said. "I mean, *that's* me, but I didn't make it!"

"Have you seen the way kids look up to him?" Lindsay said. "He's literally their hero."

"Which is the root of our problem!" Archer shouted, pounding his fist on his desk.

Lindsay shook his head. "If you send him home in the middle of the year, you'll just make him a martyr."

"I hate to say it," Duncan sighed, "but I have to agree with Lindsay. We avoid a lot of baggage if Ben finishes the year. That is, if he finishes the year *quietly*."

The silence was crushing as we waited for the headmaster to speak.

"Fine," Archer finally agreed. "Ben, you can stay, but you *won't* be back next year. And you can be sure we're wiping your mind before you go home."

"Thank you," Lindsay said.

"Oh, don't thank me yet, Lindsay. Because of your *gross* negligence, *you* are no longer head of security."

Oh, crud.

I just got Coach demoted.

Lindsay chewed his lip. "Good," he said. "The position didn't come with a pay raise anyway."

Archer dismissed me with the wave of his hand.

Coach walked me out to the hallway.

"Thanks for having my back," I said under my breath.

"Don't!" Lindsay snipped. "I told you I wouldn't be as forgiving if this happened again, didn't I?"

If my goal was to make *everyone* hate me, it was working.

"Right," I said, head down. "I'm sorry."

CHAPTER THIRTY-TWO

Valentine's Day.

A couple of weeks passed after the Power Battle was busted.

A couple of weeks of lame-o normal school as exciting as watching Chewbacca get a haircut.

No, wait, that'd actually be pretty sweet.

I was headed home at the end of the year, never to return. At first, I was heartbroken, but after a good cry, I accepted my fate. I think a small part of me wanted to just go home and forget everything.

My mind was getting wiped at the end of the year anyway, so it's not like I was gonna remember *any* of this, right?

I tried to be remarkable, and I failed.

Whatever.

The students involved in the Power Battle were sentenced to community service for the rest of the year, which meant cleaning the Lodge up and down, back and forth, inside and out.

Bathroom duty was the worst.

Guess which guy had bathroom duty.

This guy.

Lindsay meant it when he said I'd be sorry.

Dexter had become the most hated kid in school for ratting out the battle, but that kind of thing didn't bother him.

It only made him *stronger*.

And then there was Arnold.

TBH, I wasn't sure if Arnold actually knew my secret.

He hadn't said a solid word about it, and it wasn't like I could go up to him and be all,

The Braver Ravers still worshipped me, but without the Power Battles anymore, it just felt . . . wrong.

And Jennifer. I had no idea what happened to her because I had no way of contacting her. When Coach got demoted, she probably got fired.

I was never gonna see her again.

Noah, Jordan, and I were cool again, but only after I took one bite from a soggy brown apple. They said if I was really sorry, I'd do it, so I did and gagged so hard I almost barfed. I've never heard them laugh so hard in my life.

And then there was Penny. She stopped talking to me completely. She was avoiding eye contact. Turning around if she spotted me in the hallway. She even covered up the hole in her floor.

It wasn't like I didn't get it—I got it.

Plunging a thousand toilets gives a kid some time to think.

I let fame get to my head.

I was a giganto jackwad who hijacked Penny's battle.

I owed her an apology, but I hadn't gotten there yet because I was too busy feeling stupid. And I knew I needed to soon because without her, I just felt . . . *off.*

"This better be awesome," Jordan said, sporting a fancy tuxedo. "I don't get dolled up for nothin'."

"You look like a headless penguin." Noah chuckled, pushing the down button on the elevator.

The three of us were on our way to the Valentine's Day party in the banquet hall. Nothing too fancy—balloons, probably a dance floor, and definitely some red velvet cake.

When the elevator doors opened, Penny was inside. She looked like she was gonna say something, but she folded her arms and huffed instead.

I hesitated, but then I got on because waiting for the next one just would've been awkward.

Noah and Jordan didn't move.

"Are you coming or what?" Penny said to them.

"You know," Noah said, yanking Jordan's sleeve. "I forgot something back in the room."

"What?" Jordan said. "Were we supposed to bring a thing?"

Noah jabbed Jordan's arm. *"That one THING!"*

"Oh . . . *that* thing," Jordan said.

Penny rolled her eyes.

My friends weren't subtle.

The elevator doors shut, leaving me alone with Penny as Elvis Presley sang a song about the devil in disguise over the janky speakers.

"Hey," I said.

Penny stared at the floor. ". . . Hey."

"Soooo . . . *cold* outside, huh?"

"Really? Colorado's cold in the winter?"

"Yeeeeep."

Penny reached for the button for the ground floor.

"No, wait!" I said without thinking.

She stopped but didn't say anything.

Ugh! Why was this so hard?

Just tell her you're sorry!

"I, uh, I'm . . . um, so . . ." I stammered.

Penny finally looked me in the eye, and I just caved. I threw my arms around her, hugging her in a manly fashion.

She kept a straight face for about a second before buckling.

"Fine," she said, hugging me back. "I forgive you, but don't be like that ever again! You were a real knob."

"I won't!"

"And you should've let me fight my own battle!"

"I know!"

"But it's not even that," Penny said. "It's that you didn't even give me the chance! I could've *stomped* Arnold, but you jumped in before I could do anything!"

"You're right!"

"Are you even listening to me?"

"Yes!" I said. "I mean, I already know all these things you're saying! And you're right! I'm just happy to hear your voice again!"

Penny smiled.

"We good?" I said.

"We good," Penny said.

We bumped fists and blew it up.

The doors opened. Turns out the elevator never moved,

so we were still on my floor. Noah and Jordan were right outside.

"Awwww!" Noah and Jordan said together.

"Shut it," Penny said, pinching her fingers together.

The four of us went to the lobby as a team again.

It was like the stars had realigned, and everything was right in the world.

Too bad it was only gonna last for about a second.

CHAPTER THIRTY-THREE

The elevator doors slid open, and there stood Arnold waiting patiently. Dexter and Vic were behind him like henchmen.

I mean, henchman and hench*woman*.

AH, JUST THE POSER I WAS LOOKING FOR.

Vic put her foot in the doorway so the elevator wouldn't close, and then she pinned us against the back wall using her power. We struggled to get free, but it was like trying to stand up straight on the Gravitron at the carnival—impossible.

The three of them stepped into the elevator and let the doors shut behind them.

They had us cornered.

Arnold reached into his pocket and took out a stack of note cards.

Did he rehearse a speech or something?

"I have had a lot of time to think in the past couple of weeks," he said flatly. "I have even lost sleep over it, and I think it is the first time in my life that I have felt actual heartbreak."

He *did* rehearse!

"What's he talking about?" Penny asked.

"He bit me," was all I needed to say.

"When this school gave us fear, you gave us hope. You gave us strength to be ourselves—our *true* selves. But it all turned out to be a big fat groady lie. I have never felt this way about anyone before. I have never felt this much"—Arnold flipped to the next card—"*disappointment.*"

Arnold sounded like a villain, but he was 100 percent right.

Those kinds of villains are the *worst*.

"At first, I was sad," Arnold said, still reciting, "but then I just felt anger. And hatred. You lied to us. Acted like one of us, like you belonged here, but you don't, do you?"

My friends and I said nothing.

What *could* we say?

"Every single person at this school is better than you, and you know it. That is why you faked having a power. And that is why you are a pathetic loser. Your presence sullies the school, like a dirty diaper left out in the sun."

Dexter and Vic laughed as Arnold stuffed the note cards into his back pocket.

Vic let us drop from the wall.

"I'm sorry I lied to you!" I said.

"I don't care," Arnold said.

"Then what is this?" Penny said. "You stopped us just so you could give your speech? If that's all this was, then we're out."

Arnold looked at Penny and then to Noah and Jordan, disgusted. "You guys *knew* he wasn't one of us, but you helped him anyway."

"C'mon, man," I said. "What do you want from me?"

"Two things," Arnold said matter-of-factly. "One—you're my servant for the rest of the year. And two—you reject Millie's gift."

"What gift?"

"You'll see, but dude, I feel sorry for her the most," Arnold said. "Did you know she almost didn't come back to school because of what happened to her last year? She doesn't talk about it much, but she only felt safe coming back because she knew *you'd* be here, too, protecting everyone."

"I didn't know that," I said softly.

Arnold continued. "Yeah, she's *ba-nay-nay* about you, but that's why I need you to break her heart."

"But why?" Jordan asked.

"Because it'll be funny," Arnold said, like "*duh.*"

"Dude, let's just go," Noah said. "Who cares about your secret?"

"Ben cares!" Arnold said. "I don't know if you've noticed, but Ben is *more* than *just a hero* here. He's like the poster child for our future. Can you handle crushing *that* many dreams? And think of how they'll turn on you: Nobody wants a *normal kid* around threatening *our* school. Some won't care, but you'll have to watch your back for the ones who will. *Real* powers can be deadly."

My stomach turned.

My lie didn't just affect me.

It affected everybody.

Arnold laughed an evil laugh. "In a way, I'm kind of saving you by doing this. I'm showing you mercy."

Arnold and his goons allowed us to leave the elevator after that, and the four of us trudged into the banquet hall for the Valentine's Day party.

We sat at a table as students danced, laughed, and flirted all around us.

Arnold was at a table across the room, eyeballing me the whole time. Our conversation hadn't lasted long, but it didn't have to. He told me what needed to happen, and I couldn't argue if I wanted my secret to be safe.

The music stopped, and a microphone crackled. Millie's voice came through the speakers.

"Is this thing—" she said, tapping the mic. "Oh, yeah, it's on. Can I have your attention, everybody? Look up here, please?"

My heart pounded.

Did this have anything to do with Millie's gift?

"First, I just wanted to say thank you to all the students who helped with this party," Millie said. "It looks mind-obliteratingly amazing. Like, seriously, guys, two thumbs *way* up."

The double doors at the back of the room burst open.

"And second, I, with some help from the Braver Ravers, have been working on a little something to honor the bravest boy I've ever had the pleasure of knowing."

It *was* the gift.

And it was a doozy.

My fan club wheeled out a giant float of me lying on my side.

It was shirtless, ripped, and hairy.

It looked like Millie had taken Paul Bunyan's body and topped it with my head.

Penny was so flabbergasted that she kept nudging me to look, even though I already was.

"This is to say thanks for saving our lives last year," Millie said.

The applause was awkward.

Arnold nodded at me.

I took a deep breath and looked at Millie's face, beaming with pride. The statue was bizarre, but she was so proud of it.

Arnold furrowed his brow and then nodded again but faster and angrier.

"Do you like it?" Millie asked, excited.

All eyes went to Arnold as he stood, clinking a glass, rapid-fire, to get everyone's attention.

He was gonna tell my secret.

"No!" I shouted.

The eyes all darted back to me.

I swallowed hard, curling my toes. "No, I don't like it! It doesn't even look like me! I don't have a hairy chest!"

Millie laughed nervously. "Good one, Ben."

"No!" I said sternly, and then I made it perfectly clear that I wasn't joking.

The whole room went silent.

"What?" Millie's voice shook as she fidgeted

uncomfortably. "I'm, um . . . I'm sorry you don't like it, but I spent *a lot* of time on this."

"Yeah, well, it's ugly," I said, "and I hate everything about it!"

Everyone was like, "*Whoa* . . ."

Millie's voice was lost in her throat as she held back tears. Then she dropped the mic and ran out of the room.

Coach Lindsay went after her.

Headmaster Archer ordered the Braver Ravers to take the float away, and then he tried to get the party started again, but it was too late.

It was already ruined.

And I was the one who ruined it.

CHAPTER THIRTY-FOUR

Late February.

The rest of the month was awful.

Millie and the Braver Ravers hated me—no surprise there.

Arnold wouldn't stop adding to my list of chores for him—one of which was catching up on Dexter's homework that he had failed to turn in first semester. I was currently working on his report about the history of the Seven Keys.

I was in the library, at a table covered in books, when Noah and Penny showed up.

"Where's Jordan?" I asked.

"It's over fifty degrees outside," Penny said. "So he's tanning in the courtyard."

"But . . . He's invisible," I said.

"I know, right?" Penny sighed.

"Dude, take a break," Noah said. "Come eat lunch with us."

I pulled out a Pop-Tart and a Capri Sun. "I'm good."

"Why are you doing this?" Penny asked, fidgeting absently with the open books that surrounded me. "Why are you letting them push you around?"

"Because my secret might make *a lot* of kids mad," I said. "Because I deserve it for lying and cheating? Because I'm a bad friend? Because I won't remember any of this once my mind gets wiped anyway? I don't know, pick one."

"I don't think anyone'll even care that you don't have a power," Noah said. "It's not like you faked saving the school last year. *That* was real."

Penny suddenly picked up one of the books, studying it carefully. "Wait, I thought you were doing Dexter's homework," she said, confused. "Did you reopen the case of Fifteen without us?"

The case of Fifteen?

The mystery kid from orientation day?

What's that got to do with—?

Penny slid the open book in front of me.

There was a picture of Richard Kepler and his wife, Mary, on their wedding day. Richard was one of the original Seven Keys, but I didn't see how that connected with Fifteen.

"What're you talking about?" I said.

Penny took my pen and drew on the picture, giving Mary a Bride of Frankenstein beehive, and my jaw dropped.

Richard and Mary Kepler married in 1952. Donald Kepler, Richard's younger brother, was the best man.

"What the what?" I whispered. "Kepler's brother and his wife . . . *They're* Fifteen's parents? That means he's also Headmaster Kepler's nephew! Then Fifteen *was* a descendant, so why wasn't he in the yearbooks?"

"Are they still around? Maybe we can just call them and ask," Penny said, holding up her phone.

I skimmed the page. "No, it says they disappeared a month after the school opened."

"Oh, I didn't know that," Penny said.

"Me neither," Noah said. "They don't teach us what happened to the Seven Keys *after* the academy opened. Everything we know about them is from *before* that."

"Maybe he disappeared like his parents?" I said, racking my brain for the answer.

"Maybe he just never got a power," Penny said.

"Guh!" I grunted. "I wish the Kepler Cave wasn't caved in! I bet *all* the answers are down there!"

Penny set her phone on the table, and the universe slapped me across the face.

How could I have been so stupid?

"The Kepler Cave's been in Penny's pocket the whole time!" I said, snatching her phone off the table. "All we need to do is print those pictures and piece them together like a giant puzzle!"

"I can print these here!" Penny said.

"No! If this is some kind of cover-up, then we need to do it secretly so nobody knows. We need to print them online."

"Are we reopening this case?" Noah asked.

"Maybe," I said, trying not to get my hopes up. "I just wanna know who this kid is now."

Fifteen was probably a nobody.

I almost didn't care.

But at least it would take my mind off everything else.

CHAPTER THIRTY-FIVE

Early March.

I was just past the edge of the forest on the first warm day of the year.

Dexter had told me to meet him out there. Apparently, his sister, Darla, was cashing in on Arnold's deal and requested my presence for her Survivalist Club.

That meant she knew my secret, too.

Dexter was waiting for me, digging at his belly button and smelling his finger. "Put these on," he said, throwing a bag at my feet.

"What is it?" I asked.

"Darla wanted you to wear that."

"Fine," I sighed.

"Oh," Dexter said, holding up a pair of scissors. "There's one more thing Darla requested. . . ."

I gulped.

Five minutes later, I walked out to a small clearing sporting a freshly cut Mohawk and a bright orange jumpsuit that made it look like I just escaped from prison.

A white target was painted on my chest.

Probably not a good thing.

Half a dozen kids, each holding a paintball gun and wearing camouflage, listened as Darla spoke.

". . . We've practiced all year for this, cadets. Today, we hunt the greatest game of all . . . *man*."

She was talking about me.

"And can you believe he *volunteered* for this? Ben was so brave last year, and he wants us to be brave *just* like him. He's leading by example—a truly inspiring hero."

When her cadets noticed me, they clapped.

"This is super cool of you," one said. "Darla told us your psychokinetic ability keeps you from getting hurt."

"Yup," was all I said.

Darla pointed at my hair. "What's with the . . . ?" And then she pointed at my clothes. "And the . . . ?"

Dexter's donkey-laugh came from the trees.

He lied about the clothes!

And the Mohawk!

"*Let's go already!*" a girl in back growled. I caught a glimpse of her. She had a beanie on her head and a skull painted on her face.

I leaned forward to get a better look, but she kept moving, making sure the others blocked my view.

The girl in the back shouted again. "*Let's do this! Better start running, Braver!*"

I knew that voice.

I'd know it anywhere, no matter how hard she tried disguising it.

". . . Penny?"

BEN? IS THAT... OHMAGOSH, BEN, IS THAT YOU??

"Don't be like that!" I said. "*You knew it was me cuz you said my last name!*"

Penny shrugged, like, *"Yeah, ya got me."*

"You're gonna hunt me, too?"

"Dude, when will I get the chance to hunt a *human being* ever again? Besides . . . They're just paintballs."

She aimed her gun at my chest and pulled the trigger.

THOOMP!

I went down like a twelve-year-old kid getting shot at point-blank range with a paintball gun.

"Oh, that looked like it hurt," Penny said. *"Do these things hurt?"*

WELL DONE, PENELOPE! YOU WIN TODAY'S "DRAW FIRST BLOOD" AWARD!

Darla knelt by my side and showed me a stopwatch that was counting down from sixty seconds.

"What's that?" I wheezed.

Her lips curled into a smile. "Your head start."

CHAPTER THIRTY-SIX

An hour later I was covered head to toe in pine needles and paint, marching through a gauntlet of staring kids in the backyard of the school.

About five minutes into the human-hunting expedition, I had gotten snared by one of Darla's booby traps. I spent the rest of the time hanging upside down as her sociopathic club used me as target practice.

Getting pelted by a thousand paintballs from ten feet away wasn't my idea of a good time.

I was fed up.

After Penny helped me down from the trap, I went straight to my room, grabbed my backpack, and headed outside to confront Arnold and his goons.

I planted my feet firmly in front of them.

"Nice Mohawk," Vic said.

"Thanks," I said. "I mean . . . This all needs to stop."

"But we're just getting started," Arnold said.

I bit my lip. "I'm here to offer you a trade."

Arnold paused, studying me with his evil eyes. "I'm listening. . . ."

I unzipped my bag and pulled out my most treasured item, the one I had worked all summer to buy— the *only* thing I had bought with the money from mowing lawns.

It was a comic, but not just *any* comic.

"I mowed two hundred lawns in three months, working through hundreds of popped blisters, an almost endless sunburn, two instances of heat exhaustion, one heatstroke, and a visit to the ER to make enough bread to buy this," I said, presenting the comic to my worst enemy. "The Incredible Hulk #181, first appearance of Wolverine. Complete with hard plastic protective shell. It is my very favorite comic."

Arnold took my precious in his fingers. "I'm interested. What's your price?"

"You leave me alone. And you keep your silence about my . . . *secret*."

Arnold thought for a moment, and then he finally spoke. "I don't want this. I'm not an evil villain from a spy movie—I don't want *money* or *rare* pieces of art. I want *power*, and I already have that with you."

My plan kinda hit a wall when he said that.

"Hold up," Vic said, taking the comic from Arnold.

She popped the top off the plastic shell.

What was she doing?

She flipped it over, letting the book fall into her hands. And then she opened it to read the fine print.

"Dude, you got ripped off!" she said. "This isn't the original! It's a reprint! It's not even worth the paper it's printed on!"

She tossed the book back at me, pages flopping.

"What?" I said, skimming the fine print. "No, that's not . . . *I worked all summer for this!*"

My heart pounded, and my face got hot.

I was freaking out.

"I had to spend the night in the hospital!" I took a deep breath. *"I almost died for this book!"*

Arnold laughed. "Go get us brownies from the café and I'll forgive you for stepping out of line, but make sure mine doesn't have nuts. I *hate* nuts."

"Get your own brownies!" I screamed, ripping my comic in half and throwing it at Arnold.

Vic gasped. *"Whoa, I was just kidding! That wasn't a reprint!"*

Dexter honked because it was *soooo* hilarious.

Other kids looked to see what all the fuss was about.

And then something in my brain space snapped.

I dug into my backpack and grabbed Dexter's homework, laughing like a maniac as I ripped it to shreds. *"Not so funny now, is it?"*

Dexter dove at me, his skin sizzling as he powered up. He grabbed my backpack with his ice hands.

At the same time, Vic spread her fingers, aiming them at my face.

I pushed Dexter in front of me, using him as a shield against Vic's attack. He went flying but didn't let go of my bag.

My backpack burst open, and everything inside flew out.

None of my friends were there to save me.

No teachers, either.

Nobody was gonna bail me out this time.

Once Dexter got to his feet, I'd be dead meat.

He rose, steam radiating from his body as his hollow eye sockets stared darkness at me.

His fists clenched. His teeth clenched. His butt clenched.

Everything clenched.

It was entirely possible that I was about to die.

But it wasn't Dexter who finished me off.

It was Vic.

"Holy cats!" she screeched from behind me.

When I turned around, my heart stopped.

She was looking at the stat cards I had drawn in my sketchbook.

CHAPTER THIRTY-SEVEN

"*OMG, you guys! Ben created stats for us!*" Vic shouted at the top of her flippin' lungs.

Students gathered as she paged through my sketchbook, reading my notes out loud.

"*Toby's attack is only a four, but he gets bonus points if his feet stink!*"

Everyone laughed as Vic tore the paper out and tossed it over her shoulder.

"Stop!" I said, trying to grab my sketchbook, but she levitated just out of my reach.

"George's strength is that he's part wolf, but his weakness is . . . a tummy rub?"

She let George's page fall to the grass.

"Awww, you guys, did you know Penny's strength is that she's SOOO pretty?" Vic stopped and squinted at Penny's card. *"HE WROTE 'BRAVER' AS HER LAST NAME AND THEN SCRIBBLED IT OUT!"*

"*Stop it!*" I shouted again, but it was useless.

"Stay away from Liam's face because he's got nuclear dog breath! Ben marked that as a strength!"

Liam was in the crowd.

Liam wasn't laughing.

"Devin's weakness is that she needs to be liked because she thinks she's . . . ugly." Vic paused. "Whoa, dude."

The laughter turned to angry whispers as Vic went down the list.

"Dexter's IQ is his weakness. . . . Aiden's too shallow to let anything mess up his hair. . . . Emily stinks after gym. . . . Ryan's sensitive about being fat. . . . Anna will do anything for a dollar. . . . And Millie's just obsessed. . . ."

My stat cards were never supposed to be seen by anyone other than me, and they sounded *terrible* when someone else read them out loud.

My own notes were making me sick.

"What the heck is wrong with you?" Vic said, disgusted, and then she went off. *"You're judging all of us when you don't even . . ."*

Vic threw down the sketchbook and raised me off the ground with her.

I kicked wildly, but it didn't do anything. I was stuck in the air in front of a couple of dozen kids who hated me.

"Put me down!" I shouted.

"Tell everybody the truth!" Vic said.

Arnold watched from the side, satisfied and smiling.

Vic pulled at my arms like she did in the alley, bending my bones the wrong way. I swear I could hear them cracking.

"Put me down!" I said again, tears welling in my eyes.

"Tell them the truth!" Arnold shouted from the back.

I couldn't take it anymore.

"I don't have a power!" I said. *"I've been faking it since I got here!"*

The crowd gasped.

Vic let me drop.

I landed in the grass like a lump of meat.

"He's a poser!" Arnold said. "And he's taking notes on *our* weaknesses like he's *better* than us!"

I clutched my poor arms.

I wanted to defend myself, but I couldn't.

I had messed up big-time.

I started crawling, collecting the torn-out pages of my sketchbook as the crowd broke apart until I was all alone.

The remarkable Ben Braver.

CHAPTER THIRTY-EIGHT

By the next day, everyone knew I didn't have a power, but nobody cared. What they *did* care about were my stat cards, and they hated me for *those* instead.

How's that for a kick in the teeth?

Students picked on me the whole time, never letting up, during every class, every break, and every meal—picking apart my weaknesses loud enough for the whole world to hear.

I went from rock star to weirdo-eating-a-giant-tub-of-peanut-butter-alone-in-a-stairwell-after-school, waiting for the hallways to empty out so I could get back to my room without being seen.

It was the worst.

But it was all my fault.

If my parents could see me now, right?

The door was cracked open when I got back to my room.

"Hello?" I said, pushing it open, thinking maybe Noah or Jordan just forgot to shut it, but they weren't there.

Someone else had been there.

All my stuff was missing.

My clothes, my books, my comics.

Everything.

And the window was open.

I looked outside and saw my things in the grass three stories down.

Above my bed, there was writing on the wall.

"Ben Braver's weakness: judgmental jerk."

It was about 9 p.m., and I was sitting outside with Brock and all my stuff. Noah, Penny, and Jordan were with me, too.

The sky was all clouds. Good, because I didn't need the North Star to see me like this.

My friends had spent their night getting all my stuff off the grass and into neat piles next to the statue.

"Kids can be twerps," Penny said, trying to get me to talk.

"I bet it was Dexter," Jordan said.

"It could've been *anyone*," Noah said.

"*It wasn't me!*" Jordan said.

"Of course, it wasn't *you*! It wasn't any of *us*!" Penny said.

"Just sayin'," Jordan said.

It was like that all night.

Quiet, and then some yelling, and then quiet again.

They just didn't know what to say.

"I never should've made stat cards," I said.

"Stat cards are fine," Penny said. "I just don't think you understand what a weakness is."

"I wasn't trying to *judge* them."

"I know you didn't mean to," Penny said, "but you kind of did."

Coach Lindsay walked up with an old hotel dolly from when the school was still a ski lodge.

"Kids, can I have a moment with Ben?" he asked.

I had been avoiding Coach since getting scolded tag team–style in the headmaster's office.

"Sure," Penny said. "I need to check my mail anyway."

Noah and Jordan loaded my things onto the dolly and headed inside with Penny.

Coach sat next to me, and we both looked at the cloudy sky.

"Jennifer says hi," Coach said, handing me a hefty red envelope. "She wanted me to give you that."

The last time I had seen Jennifer was on Christmas Eve.

I took the envelope. "Is she okay? Is she still in the city?"

He chuckled. "Yes, she's okay, and yes, she's still there."

It was the first bit of joy I felt that day.

"She was heartbroken when I told her what happened to you," Coach said. "I think she feels partially responsible. Anyway, she gave me that and said it was for your eyes only."

I set the envelope next to me.

"I'm sorry I wasn't out there yesterday," Coach said. "It's a rotten thing that happened to you. Stat cards or not. Powers or not."

". . . But I deserved it."

"Nah. You made a mistake. I look at you, and all I see is a kid trying to keep up with everyone else, trying to fit in."

Coach got me.

"The only boy at the academy without a power. What was Donald thinking?"

I shrugged.

Coach took a deep breath. "I've been here a long time, son. Seen a lot of kids come and go. Some good. Some bad. The students here—they're *born* with powers, so they don't get it."

He stood, putting his hand on my shoulder, and looked me right in the eye.

"But I genuinely believe you're the first person who actually *deserves* one. You've *earned* the right."

Coach nodded once and went on his way.

I opened Jennifer's envelope.

A package of peanut butter cups slid out. I stuffed them into my back pocket, saving them for later. I don't know—I just wasn't in the mood for peanut butter cups.

She also included a card, and what she wrote got my hands shaking.

Project Blackwood was the Magic Lamp?

I knew exactly where that was!

I had even held it in my hands!

"Brock, old buddy?" I said. "I think I know how to fix all this."

CHAPTER THIRTY-NINE

My act 3 started with an incredibly thrilling search-and-recovery mission.

A mission so intense that it would give you nightmares during the day—*daymares!*

My own mother's child would *weep* if he heard the story of—wait, *I'm* my own mother's child.

Nevermind.

It was *way* easier to get into Duncan's lab than I thought it'd be. He had never deleted my biometric data, probably because he wasn't able to touch anything.

It was, in fact, the easiest thing in the history of all things ever. I literally walked in, ~~stole~~ *borrowed* the capsule, and left.

You'd think something as important as Project Blackwood would be way harder to get.

That sounds like a bad-guy thing to do, but the good intentions balance it out. And if it *didn't* work out, I wouldn't remember any of it at the end of the year anyway.

I booked it back to my room and slammed the door shut, thinking I'd be alone, but I was wrong.

Noah, Penny, and Jordan were there, hanging pictures on the wall.

"What're you guys doing here?" I asked, leaning against the door, feeling the weight of the Magic Lamp in my backpack.

They all looked at me funny.

"Where else are we supposed to be?" Jordan said. "It's, like, nine thirty at night."

"Plus, I got those pictures in the mail," Penny said, excited.

"What pictures?"

Glossy photos hung on the walls, pieced together like a giant puzzle. They were the pictures from Penny's phone. Our room had been eerily transformed into the Kepler Cave.

"Oh, *those* pictures," I said, feeling woozy all of a sudden.

I wasn't sure if it was because of what I had in my bag or the wall of photos in front of me.

Whatever it was, I knew I had to get outta that room. The lamp felt like it was getting heavier in my backpack, and I didn't think my buddies would be on board with the fact that I had it.

I turned the handle and pulled the door open, but only had a foot out before Noah called out.

"Dude, wait!" he said with a laugh. "Is that . . . Elvis Presley?"

"It is!" Penny said. "Or at least a kid wearing an Elvis mask!"

"Well, it *could* just be a really short dude," Jordan said.

I stopped in my tracks.

Were they being serious?

My curiosity got the better of me, and I stepped back into my dorm. When I looked at the photos on the wall, my jaw dropped.

". . . What?" I whispered.

They were right.

Dozens of Elvis Polaroids were pinned together in rows, each one a different selfie taken by the same dude in the mask.

Kepler had them strung up in his creeper cave.

Every selfie had a date written on it starting from 1963.

Each photo jumped forward a few years with the same dude in the same mask in the same outfit, all the way up to 2018. Like he didn't grow or change clothes at all for over fifty years.

And if the Kepler Cave were still standing, I knew there'd be another photo with the current year, too.

I saw it in Kepler's tenth-floor apartment.

I was *there* when the Polaroid was taken.

"I *know* him . . ." I said.

"Uh, say what?" Penny said.

"I mean, not personally, but I saw him at the beginning of the year. On the way to school, I saw him with that mask outside a diner."

My friends looked at me like I was a wack job.

"You saw *this* guy—the guy Crazy Kepler has a hundred pictures of, wearing an Elvis mask—at the beginning of the year," Noah said. *"And you didn't tell us?"*

"It was no bigs at the time!" I said. "He was just a random dude hangin' out in front of a diner!"

"Holy buckets!" Penny said, holding the class photo with Fifteen next to the photos of Elvis. "They're wearing the same outfit. *These are all Fifteen!*"

"Wait, Elvis Presley was a descendant?" Jordan asked. "This is getting hard to follow!"

"No! It's just a mask!" Penny said. "The kid in the Elvis mask is Fifteen—that's all you need to know!"

"But what's that mean?" Noah asked. "Like, if it's the same kid . . . He doesn't age? So that's *definitely* his superpower, but why isn't he in the yearbooks? *Who is he?*"

"Man, I didn't believe you guys before," Jordan said, "but this . . . This is a full-on crazy train that I don't wanna get off of."

"All these pictures, and still no name," Penny said. "The school tried so hard to make it like this kid never even existed."

Like he never existed—Headmaster Archer had threatened me with that exact same thing.

Was *I* gonna be someone's great mystery someday? Who's the weird, chubby kid in the background? They'll be bummed to find out it was a nobody.

Just then my eyes landed on the articles about the Reaper and the world ending, and I imagined the worst of the worst—a thought so vile that it made me feel like I was gonna cry.

"What if these articles aren't fake?" I said quietly, as if we were being listened to. "What if they actually happened, and the world forgot?"

Noah looked at me like I was crazy. So did Jordan. Penny, too. Okay, all three of them looked at me like that.

"What're you talking about?" Penny asked.

"What if Headmaster Kepler's nephew became a straight-up evil supervillain, and what if he destroyed these cities?"

My friends stared at me wide-eyed.

I tapped the article about the Reaper. "What if *this* is Headmaster Kepler's nephew? And what if . . . What if the world ended?"

Nobody said a word, because at that exact moment, the school's red alert went off.

CHAPTER FORTY

The hallway was crowded with students confused by the strange wailing sound coming from the PA system.

The alert wasn't a bell like the fire alarm. It was darker and creepier—like some kind of foghorn from an ancient security system. It also had an announcement telling everyone to stay inside rather than go outside.

Penny pointed down the hallway. "Is that Kepler?"

"Uh-oh . . ." I said.

The old man weaved through students while shouting at them to get out of his way.

And he wasn't wearing his hat.

"*Don't you dare make another move!*" he yelled, pointing his creepy, long finger at me.

"He already knows we know?" I said.

"That's impossible!" Noah said.

"Why else are the alarms going off?"

I ran into my dorm and stuffed Penny's photos into my bag. As many as I could in ten seconds.

It was the only evidence we had that Fifteen was the Reaper *and* Headmaster Kepler's nephew. Throw in the fact that the Magic Lamp was in my bag, and we had a pretty solid case for criminal activity.

"Now what?" Noah asked.

"Now we need to get into Lost Nation and catch the Reaper," I said.

"How do you know where he is?" Penny said.

"I don't," I said. "But we can start at the diner! Jennifer's still in town, so if we find her, she can help!"

"So you wanna catch the kid who killed millions of people?" Penny said. "Are you crazy?"

"We can't just stay here!"

"What if he's not there?"

"*What if he is?*"

Penny hesitated.

"Pen, if he's there, then he doesn't know we're coming if we go *right now*," I said. "This is a cover-up of one of the worst crimes in history. We can't just let them get away with it! We gotta do something, and we gotta do it fast!"

She looked scared, but she agreed. "Okay."

I stepped back into the hallway.

Kids were starting to panic.

You ever see a hallway full of panicked students?

It's not pretty.

The crowd was so thick that Kepler was still several doors down. We could try to make a break for it in the opposite direction, but that side was packed with students, too.

"What do I do? What do I do? What do I do?" I repeated, but then I realized my blond-haired answer was standing right next to me.

"What?" Joel said, annoyed.

I grabbed his shirt and dragged him back into my room.

"Open a portal into the city!" I said, hoisting my backpack over my shoulders.

"Are you kidding me?" Joel said. *"You're* the one he's shouting at out there! I'm not gonna help you escape!"

"There's no time for this!" Penny said, grabbing his collar.

I pointed at Jordan. "Find Coach Lindsay—tell him what we know and where we went!"

"On it," Jordan said, tearing his clothes off so he'd be completely invisible.

Penny took her uke. "I'll hold Headmaster Kepler back so you can get away."

Joel stretched a portal open over my bed. Noah and Joel jumped through first.

I glanced at Penny.

She strummed her uke furiously as a river of mice flooded the hallway full of shrieking children.

I grabbed my Braverboy cape and raced through the portal. We were in the Kepler garage. Still too far from where we needed to be.

"Can you open another portal to Campion's Diner?"

I asked. "It's, like, four miles from here. I remember the Kepler car's GPS saying that when I first drove into town!"

Joel shook his head. "I can only open portals to places I see in my head, and I don't remember that diner."

I huffed, but it didn't matter, because there wasn't any time to waste.

The three of us started running like we'd never run before.

CHAPTER FORTY-ONE

About four miles (*and the worst side cramp I've ever had*) later, the three of us were catching our breath in the alley next to the diner.

Project Blackwood, a.k.a. the Magic Lamp, was small, but it made my backpack weigh a *ton*!

The Reaper had been standing on the staircase next to the diner when I saw him take the selfie. I figured the best place to start looking for him would be in the apartment at the top of the steps.

"Hang on," I said, tying my cape around my neck.

"What's the plan?" Noah asked, frantically chewing a wad of jerky.

I shrugged nervously. "I don't know yet. Trying to focus on makin' a knot right now."

"Uh, we're going up against someone who murdered *millions* of people," Noah whispered. "We should have a plan."

"*Whaaaaaaat are you talking about?*" Joel said. "What's that even mean? Someone here murdered *millions* of people? And you're just gonna go knock on his door?"

"Yep!" I said, running up the stairs.

Noah and Joel followed.

I leaned against the railing, trying to figure out the best angle for me to kick in the door.

Do I kick the center? Or the handle?

Noah was ready with the fireballs.

Joel was freaking out.

Suddenly, a Vespa skidded to a wonky stop at the foot of the steps. It was Jennifer. I didn't know how she found us so fast, but I was happy she did.

"We know the headmaster's secret!" I shouted down to her. "He's hiding the Reaper, and we're gonna catch him!"

"Say it louder, dude," Noah said sarcastically.

Tires screeched from down the street. The headlights of the oncoming car lit up half of Jennifer's face.

"Did you hear me? I have proof that Donald Kepler is the bad guy!"

"*I heard you!*" she shouted impatiently as the car sped closer, engine revving. "*Get down here!*"

Jennifer wasn't being as cool as she should've been. She'd understand as soon as we had the Reaper in our hands.

I kicked in the door, shattering the wood at the hinges. It fell with a thump onto shag carpeting.

Noah ran in first, fireballs blazing.

I stood in the doorway, staring through floating dust at the empty living room in front of me.

Elvis had left the building.

The oncoming car's engine roared like a lion.

It was coming right toward us, and it wasn't slowing down.

"*Ben, give me Project Blackwood!*" Jennifer's shrill voice commanded.

I looked down at her rage-filled face. Her crystal blue eyes zeroed in on me like lasers.

I paused, confused. "How did you know I have it?"

At that moment, Totes's ice-cream truck plowed into Jennifer, smashing her through the wall of Campion's Diner.

As bricks exploded and metal screamed, the staircase collapsed under Joel and me, sending the two of us tumbling into the dark alley.

When I opened my eyes, everything was an agonizingly painful blur of muddy colors. A high-pitched ringing scraped my eardrums behind the muffled music of an ice-cream truck.

Noah was helping Joel up from the ground.

Good. They weren't badly hurt.

But Jennifer . . .

I stood, wobbly from the crash, my mouth tasting like dirt and blood. I hoisted my backpack over my shoulders. Couldn't lose the evidence.

Totes's ice-cream truck was smashed into the side of the diner, music still playing. What the heck was it doing in the city?

The Vespa was surprisingly untouched and still sputtering.

But all I could see of Jennifer were her legs sticking out beneath the truck like she was the Wicked Witch of the East.

OH NO...

$2

$1

$2

$3

It was like waking up to a nightmare.

I *wished* it were only a nightmare.

And then Jennifer's foot twitched.

She might still be alive!

Through the music and the haze, I hobbled over and pulled on her legs. She was impossibly heavy, but that could've been because she was pinned by the truck.

I reached under the vehicle and got a better grip, pulling as hard as I could, but her pants tore at the knees and I fell back.

I stretched my hand out again, gingerly touching Jennifer's leg, hoping it wasn't too battered and bloodied.

I stopped, confused at what I saw.

Her leg wasn't bloody at all.

In fact, her leg wasn't even skin.

It was shiny black metal.

The same wet-looking metal from Duncan's lab.

"Trutanium?" I whispered.

The passenger door of the ice-cream truck slid open, and Penny stumbled out. She reached back inside to help Jordan get to his feet.

Except it *wasn't* Jordan. It was Arnold.

Penny brought *Arnold* with her?

And then it got worse!

The music cut out, and the driver's door flopped open, but instead of Coach Lindsay—Headmaster Kepler fell out!

The old man landed on his hands and knees, barfing all over the concrete.

"I can't believe he crashed the truck," Arnold said.

"He *told* us he was going to!" Penny said. "What part of, '*Buckle up! I'm going to ram her,*' didn't you understand?"

Penny saw me kneeling by Jennifer's feet. "Ben! OMG, are you okay?"

"I'm fine," I said. "B-but Jennifer's hurt! We need to get her to a hospital!"

"*Heck to the no, dude!*" Penny said.

"What do you mean no? She could be dying right now!"

"She's *not* dying!" Penny said, grabbing my wrist and pulling me back.

"*Pen, what's your problem? Jennifer needs our help!*" I said, struggling to break free from Penny's surprisingly monster grip.

"Her name's not Jennifer!"

"*What do you mean her name's not Jennifer?*"

"She *lied* to us!" Penny said. "Her real name is Angel Blackwood!"

SHE'S BROCK'S SISTER!

CHAPTER FORTY-TWO

Penny had just dropped a bomb on me, and I couldn't believe it.

"Angel's dead!" I said. "She died in that accident with Coach's sister, remember?"

"She didn't die, though," Penny explained. "Only Olivia died!"

"How do you know?" I asked, fighting back tears. Not sure why I wanted to cry, but I kinda had a lot on my plate at that moment.

What was Penny even doing here with the head-master?

"You don't know what you're talking about!" I said. "You were supposed to keep Kepler *away*, but you *brought* him instead! He wiped your mind and made you think you needed to stop me!"

"He didn't wipe my mind!"

"Which is exactly what you'd say if you didn't know your mind was wiped!"

Noah and Joel looked at each other, like, *whaaa?*

"Our minds weren't wiped," Arnold said, nursing a

sore shoulder. "Headmaster Kepler explained it all on the way down."

"And what's *he* even doing here??" I said, waving my arms at Arnold like a loon.

"*I'm* here to actually save the day," Arnold said all pompous.

"Angel exploded in that accident," Penny explained. "Her body blew up, but her power kept her together long enough for Professor Duncan to build a suit for her. She's a walking explosion, but her armor keeps it contained!"

"What're you—*what*?" I said.

Kepler leaned against the ice-cream truck. He pointed at Joel. "You there . . ."

"My name's Joel," Joel said, a little disappointed.

"Yes, of course, I know that. *Joel*, you must open a portal back to the school."

Bricks fell from the front of the ice-cream truck as Jennifer moved under the rubble, groaning loudly.

"You must be quick! Angel will be quite unhappy when she gets up."

"Getting railed by a truck will do that to a person," Noah said.

Joel rubbed his hands together, warming them up.

More bricks fell as Jennifer reached through them.

"Posthaste, son!" Kepler urged.

Joel's fingers shook as his eyes darted back and forth between his hands and Jennifer.

Arnold rolled his sleeves up. "Let me take care of this, sir. Joel's too scared to help."

Kepler shook his head. "No, you're our *last* resort," he said. "Children, get into the truck! Quickly now!"

The five of us piled into the back of the ice-cream truck as Kepler took the wheel. He turned the key, but nothing happened.

Meanwhile, Jennifer crawled out from under the truck, her clothes shredded and her hair a mangled mess. Her eyes opened on her dust-covered face.

"Donald Kepler? Is that you in there?" she said in a creepily joyful way. "What a small world!"

"Blasted vehicle!" Kepler said, turning the key again.

The truck finally started.

The old man put it in reverse and floored it. The five of us rolled over one another in the back as the ice-cream truck flew out of the alley. It bounced into the street, then crashed into something, coming to a dead stop.

Kepler put it back in drive and slammed the pedal to the metal, spinning the wheels like crazy.

But we weren't moving.

The van tipped forward and floated off the ground. Headmaster Kepler climbed out of the driver's seat and joined us in the back.

"Stay calm," he said.

"Is it Vic??" Noah asked. "Is she outside?"

"I don't know!" I said. "I can't see anything!"

The truck tilted all the way back until it was straight up and down.

The back door clicked open, and we all tumbled out into a pile in the middle of the street.

"Be careful!" Jennifer said, dusting herself off as she walked toward us. "You could hurt one of the kids!"

"They're fine," a man said. "It'll put hair on their chest."

When I turned around, I saw Coach.

He was holding the van over our heads.

And he was totally a bad guy.

CHAPTER FORTY-THREE

Coach set the ice-cream truck on the ground gently. He must've come down after Jordan went to find—

Wait a second . . .

"*Where's Jordan?*" I said.

"He's still at the school, and he's fine," Coach said. "He thinks I came down to *help* you."

"Lindsay Andrews," Headmaster Kepler said from the ground. "You were my friend."

"I still am, Don," Coach said. "And nobody will get hurt if you just do what we ask."

My brain still didn't want to believe Jennifer was the villain.

That wasn't even possible, was it?

She was so helpful.

So kind.

So happy.

She was a sister to me!

Penny tried to stop me. She grabbed my backpack, but I slipped my arms out and marched up to Jennifer.

Her clothes were shredded, revealing more armor under-neath.

WHAT'RE YOU DOING??

"I'm sorry, Ben," Jennifer said, "but after tonight, it'll be like none of this ever happened. *Literally.*"

"But you're the bad guy?"

She shut her eyes and exhaled slowly. "I'm *not.* I'm doing this because *he's* the bad guy. His irresponsibility is what *killed* my brother."

"Brock? But Brock turned *himself* to stone!"

Jennifer gave me a look that told me to shut up.

That was it.

I was hoping that Penny was wrong.

That it was all just a giant mistake.

But Jennifer was just like Abigail—blaming her ac-tions on Headmaster Kepler.

Jennifer *was* Angel.

My anger swelled. *"You played me this whole time! Why? What do you even want?"*

Angel helped Kepler to his feet and rested him on the side of Totes's ice-cream truck.

"Are you all right?" she asked sincerely. "Can you stand?"

Kepler nodded.

It didn't make sense. What kind of villain asks the enemy if they're all right?

"Donald knows what we want," Angel said.

"It's not mine to give," Kepler said flatly.

"But you're the only one who can give it. Isn't that right, time traveler? You've changed history once—you can do it again."

Time traveler?

Changed history?

"Is your power . . . time travel?" I whispered.

"Bingo," Angel said, answering for the old man.

An atomic bomb of information exploded in my wrinkled brain as images from the Kepler Cave flashed in my mind.

The newspaper articles. Real superheroes. Destroyed cities. Millions killed by the Reaper.

My theory about Kepler was wrong. He didn't make the world forget those horrible events. He made it so those horrible events never happened.

The world *did* end.

But Donald Kepler changed history.

"I did it to save the human race," Kepler said. "But I won't do it again to save only one person."

"Three people, actually," Angel said. "You'll save Brock from turning to stone, which will save me from blowing up my car, which will save Lindsay's sister from dying in that car."

"Too many ripples. Too many things will change. Life as we know it in this moment will be altered."

Angel put her hand on her hip. "Right. Ask Abigail how she feels about ripples. She was a superhero where you're from, no? And you wasted her life by making her, what? A school security guard?"

I finally understood what made Abigail snap last year. When she saw those articles about her alternate timeline version in the Kepler Cave . . . She met the person she could've become.

"*You're* Abigail's partner?" Penny asked. "So what, you want an army to take over the world?"

"*Abigail* wanted the army, but I let her believe I did, too, to get what I wanted. She would collect students; I would control their minds. But I couldn't access my power until my suit was unlocked."

Angel picked my backpack up off the ground, reached inside, and then pulled out Project Blackwood.

Angel *Blackwood.*

"I've tried all year to subtly nudge you to find this and bring it to me," Angel said, and then she laughed.

"But subtle wasn't working, so I finally had to draw a picture of it and practically shout it at your face."

She handed me my bag.

". . . Thank you," I said instinctively.

"No, thank *you*," she said, studying the Magic Lamp intently. "Abbie's plants were supposed to find this, but they never did. The funny thing about some people . . . is that I don't need my power to get them to do what I want."

I never felt more stupid in my life.

CHAPTER FORTY-FOUR

Angel had the key to unlocking her suit, and I was the nub who gave it to her.

"That thing doesn't give powers, does it?" I asked.

"*Why* would you think it gives powers?" Kepler said, as if he weren't the crazy old man he'd been all year.

Maybe it was the hat.

"Because *she* told me that's what it was for!" I said. "*She* said you used it on yourself, and that's how *you* got superpowers!"

"And you believed her?"

"*Everybody's lying about something. I don't know what to believe anymore!*"

Penny raised her hand like it was school. "If you don't need an army," she said to Angel, "then why do you need to unlock your suit?"

"When I unlock my armor, my unstable body will explode with the force of an atom bomb," Angel said, *like it wasn't a big deal at all.*

"An atom bomb?" I said. "If that's what happens, why didn't it happen the night of your accident?"

Kepler answered for Angel. "Her suit has been containing her energy for years," he said. "Duncan warned that the pressure would build inside it and that she would need to release it periodically, but it's clear that she hasn't."

"Pretty cool, huh?" Angel said. "I'm a walking nuke."

"*Why* would you wanna do that?" Noah asked. "You'll die with everyone else!"

"Oh, it's plan B, for sure," Angel said. "If Donald doesn't save Brock willingly, then I'll force him to. He changed history once to save the world, but I believe he'd do it again to save just a small city."

I suddenly understood her diabolical plan. "You're going to blow up Lost Nation."

"He won't let it get that far," Angel said confidently.

"Don't test me, Miss Blackwood," Kepler said. "The timeline is too fragile; the ripple effect is real. It's catastrophic to this timeline—to *any* timeline. One tiny ripple in the waters of time will cause a hurricane of damage."

"That ripple mumbo jumbo only matters to someone who *knows* the future," Angel huffed.

"That's precisely why you must listen to me!" Kepler said through his teeth.

Angel paused. "You . . . *can* see the future, can't you?"

"The past, the present, the future. I know all of it."

"If you can see the future, then surely you saw all this happen tonight?"

Kepler shook his head. "My power has abandoned me in the past year. Why do you think I drove down here?"

Lindsay folded his arms, deep in thought. "Come to think of it, I haven't seen him use his power once this year."

Angel watched Kepler's face. Finally, she said, "He's lying."

"He's not changing history for you!" I said. "You need to get that through your thick skull!"

Angel turned to me, surprised. "Don't you get it? Or did you miss what he just said?"

I must've missed something, because I *didn't* get it.

"He can see the future! He *knew* Brock would turn to stone! That I would explode and Olivia would die! And he knew that you were going to jump off that building to stop Abigail, but he did *nothing* to stop any of it from happening! He did *nothing* to protect us! He just . . . let it all happen."

I wanted to argue, but . . . She was right.

Angel leaned next to Kepler. "If you knew Ben wouldn't survive the fall last year, but he still stopped Abigail, would you have let him jump?"

Kepler said nothing.

No answer was the worst answer.

"Your path was yours to walk alone, Ben," Kepler tried to explain. "Telling you *would have* created ripples that *could have* led to Abigail's winning."

I didn't think it was possible to feel worse than I already did.

But I had just been hit with the truth: I had no greater destiny.

My only job was to stop Abigail.

That's all.

Suddenly, Angel tore off her shirt, revealing the brutal truth about her body. Everything below her shoulders was encased in shiny black metal.

She set the key against a circular opening on her breastplate and twisted. Her suit came alive, small metal plates mechanically shifting to allow the key to sink halfway into her chest.

The suit glowed at the seams, burning through the rest of her clothing with precise incisions. The fabric fell to the ground, leaving her with only armor.

Two small ports popped open where her shoulder blades should've been, and pure white energy streamed like liquid from both.

She looked like an angel with wings.

CHAPTER FORTY-FIVE

We all stared as Angel's "wings" died down. She was less heavenly when they were gone.

"You all have *no idea* how good that felt," Angel said.

"*Are you crazy?*" Coach Lindsay said. "*You actually unlocked your suit?*"

The glow in Angel's suit grew brighter as she inhaled, then darkened with the exhale. "You've known me since we were kids, Lindsay. You know I never bluff."

"But . . ." Lindsay couldn't finish his sentence.

"That suit is meant to contain your power!" Kepler said.

"*I know that better than you!*" Angel said angrily. "*I'm* the one who exploded in that car! *I'm* the one you found still alive at the bottom of that ravine! And *I'm* the one who spent *months* in Duncan's lab watching him build *this* suit as my power ate away at my body. This is my *prison*."

"I credit Duncan for doing the best he could, and if you hadn't run away, you might have a more *efficient* suit right now."

Angel glared at the old man. "Save that one for Penny."

We all looked at Penny, who was just as confused as we were.

"What?" Penny said. "What's *that* supposed to mean?"

"You and I are the same," Angel said. "And someday you'll explode, too. Just. Like. Me."

Penny looked at the headmaster. "That's not true, is it?"

Kepler reluctantly nodded. "It's merely a possibility. Duncan has raised some concerns about it."

Joel took a step away from Penny.

Angel swung her arms out and spun back to Kepler. "Y'know what?" she said. "This is all pointless anyway because *you're* gonna go back in time and fix this. After that, you're gonna help me learn how to control what's inside me, which means I'll be around to teach Penny to do the same!"

Kepler hobbled closer to us. "Arnold, your reason for being here has presented itself. Godspeed."

Arnold rolled his shoulders. "Watch how a *real* superhero gets the job done," he said to me.

Arnold sprinted at Angel and then jumped at her. I think he wanted to tackle her, but he ended up clotheslining himself on her arm instead.

She grabbed the back of his shirt and lifted him into the air. Arnold twisted, grabbing her forearm and biting down hard.

He slapped his hands over his mouth.

"What did you think would happen??" Angel said, shocked. "My arm is metal, kid!"

Arnold mumbled through cracked teeth. Then he went for her face, but she immediately wrapped her fingers around his neck.

"Put him down, Angel!" Kepler commanded.

Arnold squirmed as Angel's suit shined brighter.

His eyes glowed, and his body calmed until he stopped fighting completely.

A piece of Angel's armor popped off with a *TING!*

Noah ran forward, fire rocketing from his feet as he took flight. *"Let go of him!"*

Angel dropped Arnold and caught Noah by the neck, her armor blooming once again.

Another piece of Trutanium fell off.

Noah's eyes flared as he screamed in pain. Suddenly his head burst into flames.

Angel let him drop, and he immediately calmed even though his hair was still flaming. His eyes shined so bright that his pupils were gone.

Arnold and Noah stood by Angel like they had suddenly switched teams.

She had transferred a portion of her energy into each of them. They were under her trance.

"Bring her to me," Angel said to Noah and Arnold.

The two boys grabbed Penny by the arms.

"Let go of me!" Penny said, squirming. "Noah, stop!"

Kepler wasn't doing anything to help.

"We're the same, Penny," Angel said. "Everybody has energy inside them, but you and I can *control* our energy. It's how you take over animals. And someday, it's how you'll take over people—by pushing your energy into them."

"We're *not* the same," Penny snarled.

Angel looked amused. "We are, and it's why you need to *master* your power. The energy inside you is a ticking time bomb. One bad day, and you'll explode just like I did."

Joel nudged me. I turned and saw an inch-wide portal he managed to open while no one was paying attention.

Angel lifted Penny into the air and performed her mind-control trick, but it was different this time.

Angel's energy poured into Penny, bubbling like liquid under my best friend's skin. The light within Angel's suit dimmed, her body slumping.

Penny was screaming, but no sound was coming out.

I bolted for my friend, grabbing her waist and pulling her away from Angel.

The sudden separation made Angel reabsorb all her energy at once, and she surged. The shock wave sent Penny and me flying in opposite directions—her toward Joel, and me toward the ice-cream truck, hitting it so hard that the metal dented.

More of Angel's suit abandoned her as she fell to the ground.

Joel didn't hesitate, stretching open his portal back to the school. The statue of Brock was on the other side . . . along with a second Ben Braver staring back at me.

Wait . . . what?

I looked again.

I was on the other side of the portal, at the academy, but I was also in Lost Nation?

There were two of me?

Penny's skin looked transparent as white energy bubbled underneath it. She frantically tried to rub it out.

The me on the other side of the portal grabbed Penny and pulled her through. Joel managed to escape, too, just before the portal sealed shut.

Angel stared in disbelief at her trembling metal hands. "They went back to the school!" she shouted at her hypnotized henchmen. "Find them, but don't hurt Penny!"

Noah's feet burned like jets. He grabbed Arnold by the pits and took off like a rocket, leaving all of us behind.

Coach helped Angel up. A hot mess of energy bubbled like thick slime from the cracks in her suit, dripping bright puddles onto the ground.

"Did you know I could do that?" she asked Kepler, delighted. *"Did you know I could switch bodies with her?"*

"No," Kepler answered. "But it doesn't surprise me."

Angel touched her face lightly. "I could *feel* the air on Penny's arms—the hunger in her stomach—the heart beating in her chest. Things I haven't felt since before my accident."

Another piece of her armor fell, splashing into the glowing puddle at her feet.

"You're unstable," Kepler said.

"Last chance, Donald," Angel said. "Either change history or become it."

Kepler held his ground. "I will not."

"Then the plan's changed." Angel winked at Kepler. "Penny will have to save us all."

Her body surged again, lighting up what was left of her armor. This time, I could tell, she was doing it by choice.

Lindsay ran away as fast as he could—my clue that we should probably hightail it out of there, too.

Angel was about to blow.

Kepler and I hopped onto the still running Vespa. I pulled back on the handle, and the tiny bike sputtered forward.

The speedometer went up to only sixty—probably not fast enough to drive away from an atomic explosion.

The old man shouted instructions on how to "operate a vehicle," his words.

"I know how to drive a scooter!" I said, cranking the Vespa's handle so hard that it snapped. "Oh, farts . . ."

So there we were, coasting on a dying scooter, seconds away from an atomic explosion that would take out Kepler Academy and the city of Lost Nation.

I can confidently say that was the worst day of my short, little life.

Thousands were about to die.

All my friends were about to die.

I was about to die.

And it was 100 percent my fault.

The Vespa wobbled wildly, ready to tank.

Angel exploded.

The air cracked like thunder as a wall of fire swallowed us.

Headmaster Kepler threw his arms around my waist and huddled over me, shielding me from the explosion.

And then everything was gone.

CHAPTER FORTY-SIX

Here's a question for you—if an explosion goes *BA-DOOM* and nobody's left to hear it, does it still make a sound?

Thankfully, I didn't know the answer.

Headmaster Kepler and I splashed down in an inch of freezing cold water.

It was just me and the old man.

Angel was gone, and we weren't in Lost Nation anymore.

A faint whooshing sound came from somewhere. Everywhere. I couldn't tell.

The sky was black, but not like any night sky I'd seen before. It was empty, like there *wasn't* a sky at all. It's weird, but it's the only way I can describe it—the *lack* of a sky.

Underneath me were the stars. Past the water were millions of twinkling suns amid pink-and-blue clusters of galaxies.

It looked like I was *above* all of it.

Kepler picked himself up off the ground.

We were alone and safe, but my mind was still reeling. "This is all your fault!" I said. "We were only down in the city because we know you're protecting your nephew!"

"My nephew?" Kepler said, puzzled.

"Uh, maybe you know him better as *THE REAPER*," I said. "How did you get your power? Huh? You're not a descendant!"

"Benjamin," Kepler said, rubbing his forehead. "I *am* a descendant."

"No, you're not! You came *before* the Seven Keys! You got your power *before* your brother was even experimented on!"

"Richard wasn't my brother. He was my father. And that boy you think is my nephew? He's *me*! There are two of me because I traveled back in time—one young and one old!"

"Then why doesn't he age?"

"Because he's skipping forward through time, playing a dangerous game of hide-and-seek!"

Oh.

That made a lot of sense.

I'm *such* an idiot.

The old man stumbled past me. His back looked like fried chicken from Angel's blast. I could even see parts of his rib cage.

"Holy—*are you okay*?" I said.

"I'm fine."

"Um, are you sure? Because . . ." I trailed off. I wanted to say his ribs were showing, but was there a polite way to do that? Like, when people have food in their teeth?

"I'm *fine*, Benjamin," he said, frustrated as he searched the ground.

"Where are we?" I asked, realizing I wasn't wet even though I was in water.

"Outside the universe," Kepler said, like it was nothing. "Outside of time and space."

Outside the universe?

Is that even a thing?

"The water is too murky for me," Kepler said. "What do *you* see in the reflection?"

I stared through the water. "Stars."

"Look at the *reflection*! The image *on* the water!"

I shook my head and looked again, noticing something other than my mirror image. The more I focused, the clearer it became.

I saw a faint scene of blue skies and white clouds. A city bus full of people flying through the air, carried by some kind of superhero kid with a familiar face.

Familiar because it was *my* face.

I was the kid carrying the bus . . . no gadgets, no supersuit.

It was me, and I had legit superpowers.

"What the French toast?" I said. *"Is this the future?"*

"What do you see?" Kepler asked impatiently.

"It's me, and I'm carrying a—"

"Do you see Angel?"

"No, she's not—"

"Then you're too far," he said, walking the other way past me. "Come back here and look again."

"But—"

"Benjamin, there's really no time to argue."

I ran to Kepler's side and looked at the terrifying images in the reflection.

"I see the academy surrounded by lava. Angel's there, too."

"Good, it means her blast wasn't atomic, but it will be soon. You can still save the city."

"Okay, so we'll go and—wait, just me?"

"If I return like this, I'll die," the old man said bluntly. "Time stands still out here. There's no aging and no dying."

"I'm not doing this by myself! Not after what you said about letting me jump even if you knew I was gonna die! How do I know you're not doing that again?"

"But you *didn't* die. *That's* the point!"

"But I could have! And you didn't give a flying

saucer about it! You just used me like Angel did! All to keep your precious timeline safe!"

"Surely I'm not the one pulling your strings—if it were as simple as that, why do you keep trying?"

BECAUSE I DON'T WANT TO BE ME!

I panted heavily, waiting for the old man to come back at me.

"You made me believe I had some great destiny," I said. "But it was a lie."

"I won't change things," Kepler said. "Not again."

"Why not? Just go save Brock! That'll fix all this!"

"*That* problem will be fixed, but a million others will come of it. I've spent my *entire life* keeping this timeline exactly as it is in my reflection, and I will *not* change a thing even for one student who suffered because of it!" Kepler said, spit flying. "I *saw* you jump, and *yes*, I would even *let you die* if it meant keeping the Reaper away from humanity! In *this* timeline, the Reaper hasn't returned, so it's *this* timeline I'm going to defend until my last breath!"

The old man huffed and then continued. "I've seen the end of the world, Benjamin. And it came by my own hands."

Cue the record scratch.

". . . Are *you* the Reaper?" I asked.

Kepler shook his head. "No, but we are *intrinsically* linked. All descendants are. And he used me the same way Angel uses other people. When I realized what had happened, I gathered what I could—newspaper articles and files—and traveled back to 1947 to subdue the Reaper *before* he became a threat."

"Those newspaper articles . . ."

"Yes. It happened. It *all* happened. And I started the school to prevent it from happening again."

I was blown away.

"I knew you would jump," Kepler said softly, putting his hands on my shoulders, "but I also knew you would survive. There was never any other outcome as long as I protected this timeline. I invited you to the school because you were going to save it from Abigail, but it's a decision *you* needed to make on your own. You say you don't want to be you, but it's *you* who chose to do what needed to be done. Not because of me and not because of your friends."

He was describing the kid I wanted to be.

But all this time, I was *already* that kid.

"The sad, yet wonderful, truth about the universe is that *nobody* is assigned a greater destiny," Kepler said, "which is why we must assign it to ourselves."

I got it.

Took a while, but I got it.

My path was mine to walk alone.

My friends and my family will always be with me, but in the end, my life is all about my own choices.

"Twist Angel's key counterclockwise until it stops," Kepler said. "And then pull it out. Her remaining armor will cinch together again. It won't be a perfect fix, but her power will be contained. Professor Duncan can take care of the rest after that."

"But . . . I'm scared," I said honestly.

"Being scared just means you get to be brave," Kepler said.

It was the same thing my mom had said to me before I came to school. I wonder if they planned that.

About ten feet away, something splashed wildly as it scurried our way.

"Blasted!" Kepler said. "He's found me!"

"Who?" I asked.

"The Reaper!"

The old man pushed me behind him, but whatever it was had already latched onto my leg and was climbing up my body.

I fell into the water, struggling with the invisible creature as Kepler tried to pull it off me. But we couldn't grab it.

The creature slid up my neck and over my face, suffocating me as it slipped around my entire head.

And then I heard a whisper, not from my ears, but from the inside of my brain.

"...BENJAMIN BRAVER...I KNOW YOU NOW..."

Kepler ripped the invisible creature off my head.

"Remove the key!" Kepler said, scuffling with the air.

The floor disappeared from under me, and I sank into the water.

CHAPTER FORTY-SEVEN

I fell into the middle of the lobby in the academy.

The only other person there was a Cool Beanz employee closing up shop. He looked at me for a moment and then went back to his business.

Everything else was quiet.

No creepy, honking red-alert horn.

No panicking students.

No Angel.

"*Hello?*" I shouted, my voice echoing down the halls. *"Somebody help me!"*

"You all right, kid?" the employee asked.

"Where is everyone?"

"They went back to their dorms after that weird alert thing. You should probably head back, too."

Was it possible that Headmaster Kepler brought me back early enough to warn everyone?

I ran straight for the wall and did exactly the same thing I did on the first night.

I pulled the fire alarm.

I stared at Lost Nation as the ringing bell of the fire alarm chimed behind me. Kids poured out of the academy, less groggy, but just as frustrated as they were at the beginning of the year.

"Stay inside, go outside," some kid said. *"Make up your mind, ya dumb school building!"*

My past self was still down in the city getting his heart broken by Jennifer.

Joel would open a portal soon, and . . .

Brock.

Joel's portal would open close to Brock!

That's why I saw myself earlier!

I ran to the statue, passing Duncan as he floated across the grass.

The ghost did a double take. "What're you doing here? Donald took Penny into the city to find you because you went full klepto in my lab, you little punk! Did you think we didn't have cameras set up in there?"

I stood by Brock, staring at nothing, just waiting.

"Ben!" Duncan said, angry.

"Any second now . . ."

"Any second? What're you—"

The air magically split, and Joel's portal stretched open in front of me. I made eye contact with my past self, and we stared at each other for a moment.

It was weird.

Joel dove through and landed at my feet.

"Ben?" he asked, confused.

Penny was right on the other side, white energy still bubbling under her skin. *She was pouring herself into me! She was erasing me!*

I grabbed Penny and pulled her through to the school just as the portal sealed shut.

The glow from Penny's skin disappeared. She was frazzled but all right.

Jordan slid to a stop next to us.

"What's happening?" he said. "Did Coach find you?"

"Coach is a bad guy!" I said. "So is Jennifer! I mean, Angel! Ack! I'll explain later!"

"Please tell me Angel doesn't have Project Blackwood," Duncan said.

"Wish I could. Also—she's gonna be here soon," I said. "So we need to get outta here. All of us! Everyone!"

Duncan was flabbergasted. "Where's Donald?"

"He brought me here," I said. "But he was too fried by the explosion to follow."

Duncan stopped. "What explosion?"

At that moment, the sky lit up over the heart of Lost Nation as an eerily silent ball of white energy ballooned until it burst.

The shock wave traveled through the city, shaking buildings and bending trees all the way up the mountain, streaming past the academy and bringing its terrifying sound with it.

BADOOM!

THAT EXPLOSION.

CHAPTER FORTY-EIGHT

The students of Kepler Academy gawked at the city. I looked up, afraid, desperate to find the North Star, but instead, I saw Noah fly down with Arnold in his arms.

The two of them landed in the street just past the holopods, their eyes still glowing. Noah walked to the yard and crouched, pressing his fingers into the soft dirt.

The grass around him withered, turning to ash. The earth split in front of my friend, and red-hot lava gurgled out.

Noah waved his arms like a maestro. The lava obeyed him, rising nearly twenty feet high, surrounding us all in the front yard.

He was never that powerful before. Whatever Angel did to him must've maxed out his stats. It would've been awesome if Noah wasn't a hypnotized bad guy.

Students panicked, using their powers to fight the wall of magma. Some even went after Noah and Arnold, but nothing seemed to faze them.

Arnold's eyes glowed brighter, and all at once, the Kepler students went powerless. Kids who were part animal became fully human. Jordan was suddenly visible. And Totes was a normal-looking dude pushing his shirt down because it was all he was wearing.

Duncan froze, staring blankly. "Ohhhh, please let me finally taste the sweet release of death . . ."

But he didn't disappear. As a ghost, he was somehow immune to Arnold's power.

"*Oh, come on!*" he shouted.

Headmaster Archer's voiced boomed. "Everybody stay calm!"

But he had no effect on the score of screaming kids throwing rocks over the lava wall, hoping to hit Noah and Arnold on the other side.

Penny and I caught up to Archer.

"We need to leave!" I said. *"Angel's a walking atom bomb headed for the school!"*

Nearby students stared grimly at the word *bomb*.

Archer's face was desperate. "I don't think there's anything we can do without our powers."

Things weren't looking too good.

"Hey," Penny said, touching my elbow.

I looked at Penny.

"I think everyone's waiting for *you* to do something."

She was right.

All eyes were on me, students and teachers both.

Millie was right up front. "You have to do something."

Angel was the ultimate opponent in a Power Battle. She was the final boss in a game with no extra lives and no continues.

It could've been a ranked match if I had *any* of Duncan's toys, but all his stuff was still in his lab, beyond the wall of lava.

It was just me.

Ben Braver.

I scanned the school grounds, hoping that something would come to me.

And then something did.

Suddenly I had a plan.

CHAPTER FORTY-NINE

Penny waited in the grass at the top of the small hill.
Everybody else was in place, standing in front of
her. She was the queen chess piece, and we were the, uh,
other chess pieces.

I crouched in the middle of the crowd to stay hidden.

A hole opened in the wall of lava, and Angel walked
through.

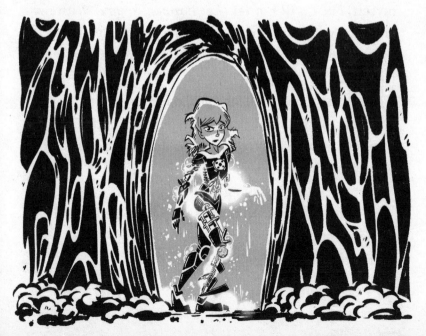

She looked worse than before. Much of her armor was missing, revealing the glowing silhouette of her body underneath.

The students in front stepped aside, allowing her to walk onto our chessboard.

"I know what you're all thinking," Angel said to everyone. "But this isn't actually my worst day ever."

I started crawling toward her.

Angel's suit dripped with energy, leaving a glowing path of white splatters and footprints.

"I used to be one of you," she continued. "A student taught to hide my power. Brock was the same, and look at us now. He's a lifeless statue, and I'm a *monster* without a body.

"*Fear* is what did this to me! I was taught to *fear* myself, *but I will not let that happen to you*! With my help, we will become a beacon for humanity! *We* will keep them safe, but we need to keep ourselves safe first!"

Angel stopped when she got to Penny.

"I'm sorry about this," Angel said. "If Donald would've listened, *everything* would be different. Nobody would've gotten hurt."

Penny blinked, staring past Angel.

"Aren't you going to try to stop me?" asked Angel. "I thought you'd put up more of a fight."

Penny remained silent.

Angel looked over her shoulder, suspiciously eyeing the rest of the unflinching students. "Why aren't *any* of you trying to stop me?"

Angel slowly reached for Penny's face, and then her fingers went right through it.

The hologram flickered.

Duncan's holopods had come in handy.

I made a dash for it, jumping on Angel's back while she was still confused. She spun, but I held tight, reaching for the key on her breastplate.

Angel grasped my neck and pulled me away.

"Ben! You're alive!" she said, genuinely happy. "But where's your precious headmaster?"

"Gone," I gasped. *"And he's never coming back!"*

"Eh," she shrugged. "I doubt that."

She squeezed tighter. I could barely breathe.

"This was a clever plan, really," she said, "but time's running short. I know you only want to protect your friend, but if you don't tell me where Penny is, then she'll die anyway, along with everyone here and in Lost Nation. It's either one person—or thousands."

I tried to talk, but my voice was strangled by her grip.

Angel looked at me curiously, then loosened up. "What did you say?"

As soon as my lungs filled with air, I shouted, *"NOW!"*

The real students of Kepler Academy stormed through the holographic wall that had kept them hidden.

Angel went down like a Jenga game as kids piled on top, her energy splashing all of us like tingly drops of water.

I finally had the key in my hands. All I had to do was twist and pull. The "twist" part worked fine, but the "pull" gave me trouble. It was stuck.

Angel tried pushing me off, but students surrounded her, holding her arms back, giving me space to work.

I planted my feet and pulled as hard as I could, but the key wouldn't budge.

And then Millie put her hands around my waist. A line formed behind her, each kid pulling the one in front of them.

The same happened on the other side of Angel, pulling her in the opposite direction.

It was a giant game of tug-of-war where the losers all die in an atomic blast.

Fun!

I felt the key give a little, and then it popped loose, sending everyone tumbling to the grass.

The lava wall fell. Noah's head rolled back, and he passed out in the street. Arnold, too. Everyone's powers came back.

We did it! We got the key out!

But when I looked at Angel, I realized it didn't work. Her armor didn't cinch up the way Kepler said it would.

I looked at the piece of metal in my hand.

It was still attached to her breastplate.

We didn't just remove the key; we'd removed the entire lock.

Angel was going to blow, and there was nothing we could do about it.

CHAPTER FIFTY

"*Everyone to the portal!*" Duncan commanded.

Students ran for Joel's open portal, leaving me alone with Angel in the grass.

Nearly all her armor was gone. She twitched like a broken toy with dying batteries. All that remained of her was a glow that boiled massive bubbles of energy. The only skin she had left burned away as her power overtook her.

My plan didn't work.

It only made things worse.

This all happened because I wanted a superpower. And now thousands would die because I stole a stupid, small chunk of metal.

"*Don't crowd!*" Duncan shouted. "*Form a line and stay calm! Trust me, we're all getting out of here alive tonight!*"

I dropped the key and ran for the portal, but Penny passed me going the opposite direction, back *toward* Angel.

"Penny, no!" I said, pulling a 180.

By the time I made it back, Angel's hand was around Penny's neck. But it was Penny who was holding it there.

"It's not working!" Penny said.

"Stop!" I said.

"It's the only way to save the city, but it's not working! She's not doing anything!"

"I can't control it anymore. . . ." Angel said. "I can't stop it. . . ."

Energy bubbled wildly around us, growing more unstable and noisy, making it hard to hear anything.

"We need to get outta here!" I shouted.

"Please . . ." Angel said. "Don't leave me. . . ."

Penny set Angel's hand down.

And then she placed her hand on Angel's head.

Penny was *staying*.

"*What're you doing?*" I said.

"*I can't just leave her! I have to try something!*"

"We don't have time to try something! Don't make me pull you out of here!"

She *wanted* Angel to take over her body.

She wanted to save the city even if it meant she'd be gone.

This was her choice.

Her battle.

I sat next to my friend and took her other hand.

She looked at me, slightly confused.

"Side by side," I said, repeating her words from the beginning of the year. "I got your back."

She smiled through tears. "You're such a dork."

She tried again, concentrating on using her power in a way she hadn't before, but it still wasn't working.

Penny let go of my hand and wrapped her arms around me. I squeezed her back, trying to tell her I was sorry, but she couldn't hear me through the whirlwind of terror swirling around us.

I made a mistake. Miscalculated. Messed up.

And it was going to cost us our lives.

CHAPTER FIFTY-ONE

"**A**ngel!" a boy shouted.

Penny and I watched his silhouette grow larger as he approached. He slowed when he saw us.

...ANGEL?

A smile appeared on Angel's face. "Brock . . . ?"

I perked up, excited that Brock was alive and talking and everything! He must've been set free by Arnold's power absorption.

"Hey, man!" I said, like we were old pals.

He looked at me. "Who're you?"

"Uh, nobody," I said. "I'm nobody. Nevermind."

Penny and I gave Brock room to sit by his sister.

He squinted as if he were trying to recognize her, and then he smiled. "You got old without me."

"You've been frozen for thirty-two years. . . ." Angel said.

Angel rested her head against Brock's chest. Even though he was only twelve years old, he was still her big brother.

"Your body . . . What happened?" Brock said.

"I lost control. All I wanted was to save you. . . . If I knew how easy it was . . . but it's too late. I never wanted to hurt anyone. . . . I made a mistake."

Brock chuckled. "Your mistakes always got us into so much trouble."

"You always found a way to fix things, though. . . ."

Brock's face twisted as his sister twitched in his arms.

". . . Fix this," Angel said.

"But your body's gone," he said. "I need you to pull yourself together, okay?"

Angel shook her head. ". . . I can't."

"Hey," he said. "Remember when you were, like, six? You used to come into my room in the middle of the night after a bad dream? You'd lie in my arms, and we'd read Garfield comics until you fell asleep?"

Angel nodded.

Energy continued to boil and swirl.

"Give me your cape," Brock said to me.

For the record, I didn't mind giving him the cape—I just wasn't thinking straight.

I untied the fabric from my neck and handed it to Brock. He wrapped it around his sister and held her close.

"Remember that one where Garfield brings a hose into the house?"

". . . And then he drenches the recliner with water?"

Brock chuckled. "Right! But then he uses a blow-dryer to dry it off!"

". . . And the chair shrunk down to his size!" Angel said.

She let out a laugh, glowing brighter than before.

Her power was peaking.

". . . You know that was the last one we read together?" Angel said. "You left for the academy the next day. . . ."

"I know," Brock said, his face twisting as he nodded. "It's time to sleep, all right?"

Angel smiled softly.

The air around us became unbearably hot.

This was it.

This was the end.

I hugged Penny close and tried to find the North Star to say good-bye to my parents.

There was a flash of light, and then . . .

Nothing.

The sky was dark, and the air was quiet.

It took my eyes a second to adjust. When I could see again, Brock was holding his sister.

Both had turned to stone.

My cape wrapped around Angel like a blanket, but the figure wasn't

the Angel we knew. It was the Angel that Brock read Garfield with—the one who fell asleep in his arms.

It was Angel at six years old.

Penny and I looked back and forth between each other and the statue.

It took us a moment to accept that it was over.

The bomb didn't go off.

And everyone was safe.

Penny flopped back onto the grass, exhausted. "All right, good game, Braver. You got some orange slices or something?"

I reached into my back pocket and pulled out the package of peanut butter cups that Coach gave me from Jennifer.

Penny took one.

I took the other.

She laid her head on my shoulder, and I rested against her. We sat in silence, eating our treat after a hard day's work.

It was melted and all smooshed up, but it was the best peanut butter cup I'd ever had in my life.

CHAPTER FIFTY-TWO

The aftermath.

Everything changed after that night.

Donald Kepler was gone. I explained what happened to Headmaster Archer and Professor Duncan, and they understood right away. I think they even expected it. Maybe Kepler told them it was going to happen since he knew the future.

They announced that Donald Kepler had died in Angel's attack—*not* that he was stuck outside of the universe.

A statue of him was even put up right behind Brock and Angel.

Brock took my place as ultimate hero of the academy, which I was totally cool with. He was, in fact, the one who saved everyone's lives by turning back to stone. His sacrifice touched the lives of all of us.

Angel's attack affected students differently. Half were *more* hard-core about honing their powers to defend themselves, while the other half just wanted to protect themselves from, well, *themselves*.

The attack messed up Penny the most. She said nothing was wrong, but it was obvious that she was afraid of becoming Angel. She even cut off all the strings on her ukulele.

Arnold and Noah were fine.

Sort of.

Arnold got his teeth fixed by the nurse with her healing power. But something was different about him. He was quieter. More of a loner. He hasn't bothered me once since then.

And then there's Noah.

No matter how hard he tried, he couldn't snuff out

the fire on top of his head. *Looks awesome*—not so practical.

The worst part? He won't be allowed to go home over the summer.

He was all, "*No big deal*," to everyone else, but I'm the only one who saw him cry because of it.

All in all, we were lucky.

Nobody was killed by the explosion in Lost Nation. Angel's blast was strongest where she stood, so everything within a half block of her was crumbs while everything past that was just rattled like a small earthquake.

A few people were injured, but nothing a short hospital visit couldn't fix.

The Lost Nation Police Department reported the explosion as accidental. No foul play suspected.

Coach Lindsay disappeared.

TBH, I hope he got away.

He was the kind of villain who wasn't really a villain. He just made poor decisions because of his love for his sister.

The more I thought about it, the more I realized that heroes and villains aren't as night and day as I thought.

Kepler's decision to change history gave a sad ending to a lot of people, but he did it to save the world.

Abigail only wanted to help humanity with her power.

Even Angel just wanted her brother and her body back.

The only one acting selfish and stupid this year . . . was me.

Was I the bad guy in my sequel?

I took all my stat cards, scribbled out the weaknesses section, and then hand-delivered them to their owners along with a short "I'm sorry for being a wad" speech.

It didn't erase my mistake, but it was a start.

Millie forgave me, so that was cool.

She wasn't a fan anymore.

She was a friend.

The biggest bummer was that I was done at the academy. Headmaster Archer told me I wouldn't be attending eighth grade there. It was my consequence for stealing Project Blackwood and giving it to Angel. And also, like, the million other rules I broke while I was a student.

But the good news? My mind wasn't going to be wiped. I'd remember everything. The school. My friends. My adventures.

Headmaster Archer said he hated the idea of wiping minds. He considered it a policy of the old leadership and felt it was time for change.

One thing was for sure.

Kepler Academy was never going to be the same.

CHAPTER FIFTY-THREE

My last day of school.

My last day at the academy.

My last day with my best friends.

Forever.

The graduation ceremony was scheduled after Donald Kepler's memorial service, with both taking place in front of the school. A giant portrait of him watched students from the stage.

Several professors shared memories they had of the old man, but none of them shed a single tear. Funerals are supposed to be sad and awkward. It was almost like people couldn't wait for this one to end.

My friends and I sat in the last row.

"Can't believe they're saying he's dead," Penny said. "Not after what you told us."

"They thought it was better this way," I said.

"Just more adults pretending something didn't happen," Noah said, head crackling like a campfire.

"What did it look like out there?" Jordan asked. "Outside?"

"Like I was standing on top of the universe," I said. "Because I think I *was*."

"I bet if we took the nurse out there, she could heal him," Noah said.

"Maybe, but I think *he's* the only one with the power to go out there. It's not like there's an elevator with a button for the outside of the universe."

Another teacher took the mic and started in with a boring story about the old headmaster, but she was interrupted by a loud crash on the stage.

Students stood on their chairs, making it impossible

to see what was happening from the back row, but I could hear it over the speakers.

We ran down the aisle to get a better look.

A kid was writhing around on stage, frantically attacking his own head, looking exactly like I did when I was Outside—when that *thing* suction-cupped my head.

And then he stopped.

I got a good look at the boy's face.

Actually, I got a good look at his *mask*.

It was Elvis Presley.

The boy tore off the mask and tousled his black hair. A Polaroid camera hung from his neck.

When he saw Headmaster Kepler's giant portrait, he blew a raspberry and pouted. "I'm at my *funeral?*" he said, his face turning from disappointed to glee. He raised a fist. *"That means I wiiiin! Hide-and-seek champion of the universe!"*

Headmaster Archer approached slowly. "Young man, are you . . . lost?"

"Nope," the boy said.

"Do you know where you are?"

The boy didn't answer. Instead, he jumped from the stage and strolled back to the school like he owned the place.

"That statue's boss!" he shouted over his shoulder as he passed Brock and Angel. "The one of the old skuzz is a little on the nose, though."

Students mumbled, trying to figure out what was happening, but my friends and I already knew.

It was the kid we had been investigating all year.

The one who was there on orientation day and then disappeared. It was the kid who skipped forward through time, playing hide-and-seek with the older version of himself.

It was Elvis.

It was Fifteen.

It was the eleven-year-old Donald Kepler.

He had just dropped in from the Outside, wrestling an invisible creature on his head—the same one I wrestled with when I was Outside.

It was the villain who ended our world in an alternate timeline.

It was the Reaper.

And now he was back in *our* timeline.

HOLY DONKS.

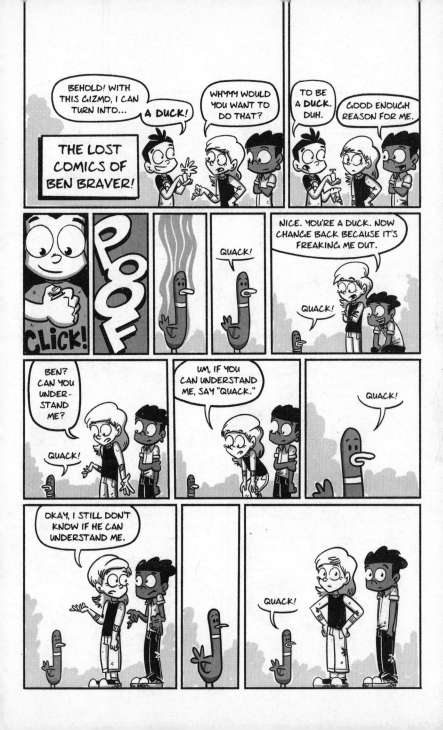

ACKNOWLEDGMENTS

Thank you to all the readers who jumped into this book and took the adventure with Ben!

To everyone at Roaring Brook Press who helped bring this book to life. To my talented editor, Connie Hsu, for your dedication and enthusiasm toward this series, and for pushing Ben to be more than a cartoon character. To Megan Abbate for navigating me through a story full of mystery and for your endless support. To Aimee Fleck for being so good at what you do.

To my agent, Dan Lazar, for all the round-the-clock communication to get me to the place I am today. To Torie Doherty-Munro, Cecilia de la Campa, and every-one at Writers House for all your very hard work.

To Camye, for your incredible patience and for being the sounding board to all my dumb ideas. To Evie, Elijah, Parker, Finn, and Adler for hanging out with me while I work.

And last but not least—Bastian Bux, Elliott Thomas, Dr. Henry Walton (Indiana) Jones Jr., Gizmo, and Captain Jean-Luc Picard.

Will Donald Kepler be trapped Outside forever?

Will the Reaper get his revenge?

And will Professor Duncan ever taste
the sweet release of death?

Keep reading for an excerpt.

You see that?

That . . . is a black hole.

Or something like it.

It was more like a giant vortex of doom that was growing larger smack dab in the middle of Times Square in New York City. Not the best place for something like that to randomly appear, but that was the point.

It was one of those "end of the world" moments that always happen in movies. No superhero battle is complete without a massive hole of death in the sky, threatening all life as we know it, right?

Yup. That thing was gonna tear the planet apart. I'd love to tell you I had nothing to do with it, but I think you know me better than that by now.

I might be a *little bit* responsible for it.

But only a little.

I wanted to save the day, but instead, I set off a chain reaction that was about to lead to the extinction of the human race.

Whoopsies . . .

CHAPTER ONE

My name is Ben Braver, and I am a *nobody*.

For you noobs out there, here's the deets . . .

Two years ago, I was invited to Kepler Academy for sixth grade.

It's a super-secret school for super-secret kids with super-secret superpowers. The whole thing was super-secret. Obviously, I accepted the invite—because who could say no to that?

I was pumped!

Was I invited because I had a power?

Was I gonna *get* a power?

Was I gonna be *the Chosen One*?

The answers to those questions are nope, even more nope, and nope with some extra salt.

Turns out, the only people in the world who have powers are those born with them. And they're all descendants of the Seven Keys—seven peeps who were experimented on in a laboratory. None of them got powers, but their kids (a.k.a. "the descendants") did. And since I'm not a descendant, I'll never have any powers.

Bummer, right?

So why the heck was I invited to the academy at all?

Because I was destined to save the school.

Twice.

Turns out the headmaster, Donald Kepler, is a time traveler, and he saw a future where his academy needed a no-powered nobody like me.

He had seen a future where the world ended, destroyed by some jerk named the Reaper. But it didn't end, because Kepler changed history—and trapped the Reaper outside the universe so he could never ever become the bad guy. Kepler spent the rest of his life protecting this timeline from that terrible fate.

But now, I'm at Kepler's funeral.

And the Reaper?

He's back.

CHAPTER TWO

Ten hours ago...

So there I was, sitting in the last row at Headmaster Kepler's funeral on the very last day of seventh grade, roasting marshmallows on Noah's head. His hair had gone full Human Torch a few months back, and nothing he did could snuff it out.

Penny and Jordan were chillin' on the other side of me. You see Penny's arm around my back?

Yeah, no, I just wanted you to see.

It's not around *Jordan's* back.

Just sayin'.

Anyway, those three are my BFFs, but sadly, I knew it was the last day I'd ever get to hang out with them.

The school year was over, and in just a few hours, I'd be on my way back to my parents at home, never to return to Kepler Academy.

Don't get me wrong, I *wanted* to go home. As far as the school? I was over it. Too much danger for *this* kid.

I mean, I had almost *died* there.

Like, a *hundred* times.

But I wasn't ready to leave my friends.

Not yet.

We were all decked out because that's usually how it goes for funerals. At least I think it is. I'd never actually been to one.

Technically, I still haven't, because Kepler wasn't exactly dead. He was badly injured after saving me from a horrible explosion. If he'd stayed in our world, he would've died, so he escaped outside the universe. Now he's stuck there, alone in a place where time doesn't exist.

I'm still alive because of him.

And I never got the chance to say thanks.

Onstage, one of the teachers took the mic and started

in with a boring story about the old headmaster, but she was interrupted by a loud crash.

I got this gross feeling, deep in my gut—the kind that tells you to run away because something terrible is about to happen.

I'm really good at ignoring that feeling.

Students stood on their chairs, making it impossible to see what was happening from the back row, but I could hear it over the speakers.

I jumped up from my seat and tore down the aisle.

"Ben, wait!" Noah said. "What're you doing?"

"Getting a better look!" I said.

I stopped in front of the stage. On the center of it was a kid wearing an Elvis Presley mask, writhing around like he was wrestling something invisible.

And even though I couldn't see it, I knew what it was because the same thing tried to suction-cup itself to my head a couple months ago.

It was an invisible creature that ended the world in an alternate timeline, a.k.a. . . . the Reaper.

And then the kid stopped.

He ripped off the Elvis mask, frantically searching his body for whatever had been clinging to him, but when he shrugged it off, I knew it was too late—the Reaper wasn't on him anymore.

And it was obvious that the kid had no idea what he had just wrestled with—if he did, he'd be freaking out just as much as I was, but he was totally calm.

When he saw Headmaster Donald Kepler's portrait, he blew a raspberry and pouted. "I'm at my *funeral*?" And then he raised a fist.

The new headmaster, Raymond Archer, approached slowly. "Young man, are you . . . lost?"

"Nope," the boy said, vigorously rubbing his head once more to check for the invisible creature.

Still nothing.

The boy jumped from the stage and strolled back to the school like he owned the place.

Students mumbled, trying to figure out what was happening, but I already knew—it was Donnie Kepler, the eleven-year-old version of Headmaster Kepler. Donnie had been skipping through time, playing hide-and-seek with the older version of himself, and now he was here.

And he had accidentally brought the Reaper with him.

"Holy donks," I whispered.

I pulled my shirt over my head to protect myself and

frantically started searching for the invisible creature that was most *definitely* nearby.

My friends caught up with me as Headmaster Archer ran to the school, disappearing through the front doors.

"Bro, you gotta stop running off like that," Noah said. "Next time, wait so we can come up with a *plan*."

UMM, WHAT'S WITH THE TURTLE IMPRESSION?

My friends didn't realize the Reaper was with Donnie. They'd FREAK OUT just as much as I was if they knew. But it didn't matter because Penny was *clearly* freaking out, too.

She yanked my shirt down and stared at me with the fire of a thousand suns burning in her eyes. "What's wrong?? You're acting like something *horrible* is happening!"

I wanted to tell her everything. To tell her that the monster who destroyed the world was literally standing around us somewhere, probably thinkin' about destroying the world again.

But I couldn't.

Because, at that moment, the Reaper didn't know I knew he was there, which meant I had the upper hand.

I needed to get to Donnie. He was wrestling that thing when he bounced on the stage.

"I need to get to Donnie," I said. "Where'd he go?"

Noah pointed to the front of the school. "He's up there."

Donnie was at the buffet tables that had been set up for the funeral lunch. He was putting food on his plate like he *didn't even care* he'd brought the apocalypse with him.

Did he even know??

I was about to run to Donnie but stopped because Penny looked like she was about to have a meltdown. She was whipping her hands like she was trying to shake water off them.

"Are *you* okay?" I asked.

"*Don't worry about it!*" she said, mocking me, and then she shoved her hands into her pockets. "I'll catch up! Just go without me!"

She didn't have to tell me twice, so I started running.

"Ben, come on, man!" Noah said, annoyed. "*Do you hate plans or something?*"

None of the kids working the buffet tables seemed to care that Donnie was grabbing some grub, except for Dexter and Victoria—the academy's unofficial bullies. They were helping with the lunch setup, but only because it gave them first dibs on all the food. They glared at Donnie as he carefully stacked potato chips on his plate.

I stopped a few feet from him, not sure what to say.

"You guys still eat hot dogs in the future," Donnie said, grabbing one with his free hand. "That's so *lame.*"

"Why?" Vic asked.

"I just expected *more*," Donnie sighed. "Where are the flying cars? The floating cities? I mean, do you guys even live on the moon yet?"

Vic stared at the boy. "Who *are* you?"

"Donnie Kepler."

"No," Dexter said. "Donald Kepler's *dead.*"

"Right. *That* Donald Kepler's dead," Donnie said, nodding toward the funeral. "But *I'm* not."

Dexter and Vic looked like confused mules.